She got the impression he had been standing in the doorway for some time studying her.

His dark hair was wet, and water beaded on the dark curls of his chest hair that formed a *V*, disappearing into the towel wrapped around his slim hips.

"I'm sorry, the door was open," she said quickly.

He was as big a man as she'd first thought, a few inches over six feet and broad at the shoulders. Solid looking, she thought. Not like a man who worked out. More like a man who worked.

He settled those dark eyes on her. Everything about him was dark.

"You're new here," Cade Jackson said, as if roping in his irritation. "You don't know me, so I'm going to cut you some slack. Get out. I don't know what your game is, Tex, but I'm not playing."

B.J. DANIELS

CLASSIFIED CHRISTMAS

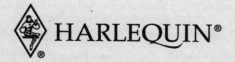 HARLEQUIN®

TORONTO • NEW YORK • LONDON
AMSTERDAM • PARIS • SYDNEY • HAMBURG
STOCKHOLM • ATHENS • TOKYO • MILAN • MADRID
PRAGUE • WARSAW • BUDAPEST • AUCKLAND

This one is for Jody Robinson, for her encouragement and support and friendship.

ISBN-13: 978-0-373-69297-2
ISBN-10:   0-373-69297-8

CLASSIFIED CHRISTMAS

ABOUT THE AUTHOR

B.J. Daniels's life dream was to write books. After a career as an award-winning newspaper journalist, she sold thirty-seven short stories before she finally wrote her first book. That book, *Odd Man Out*, received a 4½ star review from *Romantic Times BOOKreviews* and went on to be nominated for Best Harlequin Intrigue of 1995. Since then she has won numerous awards, including a career achievement award for romantic suspense.

B.J. lives in Montana with her husband, Parker, two springer spaniels, Spot and Jem, and an aging, temperamental tomcat named Jeff. When she isn't writing, she snowboards, camps, boats and plays tennis.

To contact B.J., write to her at P.O. Box 1173, Malta, MT 59538, e-mail her at bjdanielsmystery@hotmail.com or check out her Web site at www.bjdaniels.com.

Books by B.J. Daniels

CAST OF CHARACTERS

Cade Jackson—For the first time in years the cowboy was looking forward to Christmas. That was until Andi Blake showed up in town.

Miranda "Andi" Blake—The new reporter in town stumbled onto the story of a lifetime. Unfortunately it put her not only in danger, but also in the arms of the last man in Whitehorse she should get close to.

Grace Browning Jackson—Her greatest fear was that her secret would come out. Even after her death.

Houston Calhoun—It was no surprise he took to a life of crime, having been born into a family of bank robbers.

Lubbock Calhoun—He's been waiting to get out of prison and finish what he started in Whitehorse.

Bradley Harris—The newspaper fact finder was a reporter's best friend—especially Andi Blake's.

Arlene Evans—The mother of three was worried she wouldn't live to see her children raised, because at least one of them still wanted her dead.

Violet Evans—Arlene's eldest daughter was making plans for her return to Whitehorse.

Charlotte Evans—Arlene's youngest couldn't believe her mother hadn't noticed the little secret she was carrying.

Chapter One

This year was different. Cade Jackson couldn't swear why exactly, just that he wasn't anticipating the anniversary of his wife's death with as much dread.

Maybe time *did* heal. Not that he didn't miss his wife. Or think of her. Especially with the anniversary of Grace's death only days away. He just didn't hurt as much when he thought of her. Nor after six years did he think of her as often.

There was something sad about that, he thought, as he watched the other ropers from the top rung of the corral. The thunder of hooves raised a cloud of dust that moved slowly across the enclosed arena.

Outside, snow continued to fall, promising a white Christmas. He breathed in the comforting scent of leather and horses, both as natural to him as the lay of the land beyond the arena walls.

Snow-covered open prairie ran to the deep cut of the Missouri River as it wound its way through Montana, the dark outline of the Little Rockies that broke the horizon.

He felt as if he'd come of out of a coma. Everything looked and smelled and felt new and different. He'd missed a lot of holidays with his family, lost in that dark place that his grief had taken him. But this year he felt as if he might make it through the holidays without having to hide out at his cabin or in his ice-fishing shack until Christmas was over.

Cade felt an odd prickling just under his skin and looked toward the window. Snow fell in huge flakes that floated down blanketing the earth with both cold and silence. He frowned at the sudden sense of apprehension he'd felt just moments before. What had that been about?

He shook it off. He wasn't going to let the old ghosts get to him. He was finally feeling as if he might make it.

ANDI BLAKE discovered a manila envelope on her desk when she got back to the newspaper from lunch. She'd spent her first morning at the *Milk River Examiner* cleaning off her predecessor's desk, only a little unnerved by the fact that he'd been murdered, thus the opening.

Glen Whitaker hadn't been neat. After boxing up all of his notes, she'd cleaned the desk, scrubbing away months if not years of grime.

She gave the envelope only a sideways glance as she slipped off her jacket and hung it over the back of her chair.

The envelope was addressed to her and had a White-horse postmark. Nothing unusual about that except for the fact that it was addressed to Andi *West,* the name she'd gone by as a television newscaster in Fort Worth, Texas.

She felt a shiver of trepidation. No one here knew her

as Andi let alone Andi West. Her full name was Miranda West Blake. She had been named after her father, Weston Blake. He was the one who'd nicknamed her Andi.

To put Fort Worth and the past far behind her when she'd applied for this job though, she'd used Miranda Blake and now wrote as M. W. Blake.

She'd thought by moving to Whitehorse, Montana, and using her real name that she would be able to escape from the terror that had run her out of Texas. Had it followed her?

Her heart pounded. All her old fears came back in a wave of nausea. Was it possible there was nowhere she could get away from it?

Fingers trembling, she picked up the envelope, turning it in her fingers. The contents felt light. And the package didn't sound like it was ticking. Something slid inside making her jump.

Her fear, though, gave way to anger. She was sick of being scared. She'd given up everything she loved because of some psycho. If he'd found her...

Taking out her letter opener, she sliced through one end of the envelope and carefully dumped the contents onto her desk.

She'd gotten enough of these at the television station that she knew what to expect.

A white cassette tape thudded to the desktop an instant before a piece of newspaper fluttered down beside it, surprising her.

She frowned and picked up the tape. It was file-card size. There was nothing written on it. She glanced at the

CD player on her desk and wondered where she might find a cassette player that played this size tape.

Not that she would play it. She'd learned it was better not to listen to the calls although she'd read most of the letters before handing them over to the police. Except the police hadn't been able to find her stalker let alone stop him or the threatening letters and calls.

Putting down the tape, she turned her attention to the other item from the envelope. As she unfolded the newsprint, she saw that it was a clipping of a local newspaper brief about a woman named Grace Jackson who'd died in a one-car rollover south of town.

She felt a wave of relief. Apparently someone thought the story warranted a follow-up. That's all this was.

True it was odd because the accident had happened six years ago Christmas Eve.

But at least it wasn't connected to Texas. Or her. She tried to relax.

Still the fact that it had been sent to Andi West bothered her. Who besides the newspaper publisher, Mark Sanders, knew her television name?

Just then Mark Sanders came in the door.

She held up the clipping and he took it from her as he walked by her desk, glanced at the story and handed the clipping back saying, "Yeah, that was real sad. They hadn't been married long." He started to walk off.

"Do you want me to do a follow-up?" she asked his retreating back.

He stopped to glance over his shoulder and frowned. "Can't see any reason. It's been what—"

"Six years," she said.

"Right. No reason to bring it back up," Sanders said.

"Someone sent it to me."

"Just file it. You're covering the Parade of Lights tonight, right? It's a pretty big deal in Whitehorse. You sure you don't mind shooting it, too?"

"No problem." She didn't bring up the name thing. It was possible, she realized, that Mark Sanders had told someone who she was thinking no one in Whitehorse, Montana, would care let alone cause her any trouble.

"I've got it covered," she assured him, imagining what her best friend back at the television station in Fort Worth would say if he knew she was covering parades for a small-town weekly newspaper, taking the photographs as well as writing the stories.

She hadn't talked to Bradley since she'd left Texas. Maybe she'd call him. She was sure he was probably worried about her since he'd tried to talk her out of coming up here. She missed him and hadn't wanted to call until things were going better. She didn't want to hear him say I-told-you-so. Even though he was right. She feared this move had been a huge mistake.

But she had some time to kill before the Parade of Lights and she really needed her friend.

"Hello?"

Just the sound of Bradley's voice brought tears to her eyes.

"Hello?" The apprehension she heard in his voice surprised and worried her.

"It's me," she said quickly. "Are you all right?"

"Hey." Instantly he sounded like his old self again. "I'm fine. I just thought it was someone else calling. I've been getting some obscene telephone calls. I might enjoy them if I was straight," he said with a laugh. "I am so glad you called. I have been worried to death about you. I was beginning to think you'd forgotten about me."

"No chance of that," she said, tucking her feet up under her. It was almost like old times talking with him over a delivery pizza and old movies.

"So how bad is it?" he asked.

"It's…interesting."

"I told you not to take that job. You must be bored to tears. You haven't been banished, you know. You can get on the next plane and be back in Texas in a matter of hours. I'll pick you up at the airport."

She laughed. It *was* tempting.

"So how horrible is it in the wild, wild West?" he asked. "You can tell me."

"It's freezing cold for starters."

"I know. I confess I've been watching the weather. I knew you were going to freeze your cute little behind off." He laughed. "Seriously, how are you?"

"Homesick for you, for warm weather, for Mexican food." She smiled. "There isn't any in Whitehorse."

"Imagine that," he said with a smile in his voice.

"So how are things at the station?"

"It's been bloody hell. There was practically a revolt over your job even though everyone knew the position was only temporary."

Her boss had promised to hold her job for six months.
"So who got it? Anyone I know?"

Bradley let out a dramatic sigh and she knew.

"Rachel," she said. Rachel was as close a female
friend as she'd had at the station. "I'm happy for her."

"Oh, please," Bradley said. "You can be honest. It's
me, remember?"

Andi laughed. It felt good. "You're just jealous
because she won't let you try on her shoes."

"I miss you."

"I miss you, too." She hated to ask, but she had to. "Has
the station received any more threats addressed to me?"

That telltale beat of silence, then, "I made sure they
were turned over to the police."

Hearing this surprised her. She'd thought the threats
would stop once she wasn't on the air anymore.

"I'll bug the cops until they find this freak and lock
him up so you can come home."

She smiled through her tears. "You're a good friend."
She hung up, glad she'd called him. She felt better about
her decision to come to Montana. If the television
station was still getting threatening letters for her, she
was much better off being as far away from Fort Worth
as she could get.

As she started to file away the news article about the
woman who'd died in the single-car accident, she
stopped to read it through again, still curious why
anyone would have sent it to her.

The deceased woman, Grace Jackson, had apparently been driving at a high rate of speed when she'd lost

control of her car south of town. The car had rolled numerous times before landing in a ravine where it had caught fire.

As she had the first time she'd read it, Andi shuddered at the thought of the poor woman being trapped in the vehicle and burning to death. There were so few vehicles on the roads up here and miles between ranches let alone towns. Even if the car hadn't burned, the woman probably would have died before someone had come along.

According to the article, Grace Jackson had been married to a Cade Jackson. Wasn't the sheriff's name Jackson? Carter Jackson, as she recalled from reading back papers to familiarize herself with the town.

She wondered if Cade and Carter were related. Pretty good chance given their names. The sheriff's name had come up quite a lot in the news—including the murder of the reporter who'd had this desk, Glen Whitaker.

She looked again at the manila envelope the newspaper clipping and tape had come in, checking to make sure there wasn't a note that she'd missed. Nothing. The envelope had been mailed in Whitehorse so at least it was from someone local.

She filed the story, still a little anxious, though, that at least one person in town knew her other name.

As she pocketed the cassette tape, she wondered where she could find a tape player.

THE PARADE of Lights definitely was an event in Whitehorse, Montana. Andi stood on a curb with the rest of the county that had turned out, everyone bundled up for the cold, snowy December night, as one homemade float after another cruised by.

The air was filled with excitement, the stores along the main street open and lit brightly for the event. The smell of Christmas trees, hot cider and Native American fry bread wafted in the chilly air.

The streets were packed with not only townspeople, but also apparently ranchers and their families had come in from miles around for the event.

Andi shot a dozen photographs of the floats, surprised at how many there were given the temperature and how much work had gone into some of them.

She liked the small-town feel, which surprised her. It felt like an extended family as she heard people visiting and calling greetings from the floats.

Just as she was finishing up, she heard someone call out, "Cade!"

She looked up to see an attractive woman waving from one of the floats. Andi followed the woman's gaze to a man leaning against the building yards to her right. She could see only his profile, his face in shadow under the brim of his Western hat, but he was tall and all cowboy. He wore boots, jeans, a sheepskin coat and a Stetson, the brim pulled low, dark hair curling out from under the hat at his nape.

From the way he stood, back in the shadows, she got the impression he had hoped to go unnoticed.

Cade *Jackson?* The husband of the deceased woman from the newspaper clipping?

Andi lifted the camera and impulsively snapped his photograph. As she pulled the camera down, he disappeared into the crowd.

Cold and tired, she returned to the newspaper office just down the block, anxious to get her photographs into the computer. Warmer, she decided to go ahead and write up her story even though it was late.

She knew she was just avoiding the small apartment she'd rented on the other side of town. It wasn't far from the newspaper given that Whitehorse was only ten blocks square. She usually drove to work out of habit more than necessity, although she didn't relish walking through all the snow.

The apartment was small and impersonal to the point of being depressing. In time she would make it hers, but right now she preferred the newspaper office to home.

After she put in the photographs and wrote cutlines for each, she sat down at the computer to write an accompanying article.

Her mind wandered, though, and she found herself calling up the photograph of the cowboy she'd seen on the main street tonight, the one the woman had called Cade. How many Cades could there be in Whitehorse?

The publisher had said Cade Jackson and his wife, Grace, had only been married a short period of time before her death. That meant there should be a wedding announcement in the file, she thought, unable to shake her curiosity as to why someone had sent the cassette and clipping to her.

Five minutes later, she found the wedding announcement and photo. The two had married November 14—just weeks before her death.

Andi studied the photograph of the groom, comparing it to the one she'd taken of the cowboy she'd seen on the street tonight. Cade Jackson. The two were one and the same.

The cassette was still in her pocket. Now more than ever she was anxious to find a player and see what was on the tape.

Intent on the cowboy, Andi finally looked at the wedding photo of the bride, Grace Browning Jackson. Her mouth went dry, her heart a hammer in her ears.

She *knew* this woman.

Except her name hadn't been Grace Browning. Not even close.

Chapter Two

Andi Blake stared at the photograph, telling herself she had to be mistaken. But she knew she wasn't.

It *was* Starr, she'd stake her life on it. Starr Calhoun wasn't someone she could have forgotten even if the first time Andi laid eyes on her wasn't indelibly branded on her memory. They'd both been only young girls. Andi remembered only too well the look they'd shared before all hell broke loose.

And it wasn't as if Andi hadn't seen Starr Calhoun since, she thought with a chill.

It made sense, Starr masquerading as this Grace Browning woman and marrying a local yokel. Starr Calhoun had been hiding out here, using marriage as a cover, waiting. Waiting for what, though?

Her brother Lubbock! He'd been arrested only an hour away from Whitehorse six years ago. She felt a chill as she realized she was meant to come here. As if it had always been her destiny. As if Starr Calhoun had called her from the grave.

She shivered and glanced toward the front window of the newspaper office along the main street, suddenly feeling more than a little paranoid.

A few shoppers straggled past. The Christmas lights still glowed in the park across the street by the train tracks. Next to the old depot, a half dozen passengers waited by their suitcases. Whitehorse's depot had closed years ago, but a passenger train still came through. Passengers had to call for tickets and wait outside until the train arrived.

Andi got up and closed the front blinds, double-checking the front door to make sure she'd locked it.

It didn't take her long to find a more recent photograph of Starr Calhoun on the FBI's most wanted list. She printed the photo, standing over the printer as it came out. The copy wasn't great. But then the original had been taken from a bank surveillance camera.

That had been six years ago August. Wearing masks and carrying sawed-off shotguns, a man and woman had robbed a series of banks across Texas amassing an estimated three million dollars over a two-week period.

During what turned out to be their last robbery, there had been an altercation and the mask Starr Calhoun had been wearing was pulled off by a teller exposing her face to the surveillance camera.

A warrant had been issued for Starr Calhoun, but she and her accomplice had gotten away and had never been heard from again. Nor had the money been recovered.

The accomplice was believed to be her brother Houston Calhoun, a known criminal who'd done time for bank robbery.

The Calhoun family shared more than their distinctive pale blue eyes and curly auburn hair. Nor was the robbery six years ago the first time Starr Calhoun had been caught on a bank surveillance video camera.

She was first filmed at the age of three when her infamous parents Hodge and Eden Calhoun hit a bank in Orange, Texas, with all six children in tow ranging in age from fifteen to three.

Hodge and Eden had eventually been caught, their children put into foster care and scattered to the wind.

Andi made a note to find out the latest on the rest of the Calhouns. At least she had a good idea where Starr had disappeared to, she thought, studying the wedding photograph.

She couldn't help the small thrill she felt. Her instincts had been right. As a reporter, she'd made a point of keeping track of the infamous Calhoun family. Whenever a news story from any part of the country mentioned one of the Calhouns, her computer flagged the story for her.

That's how she'd seen the article about Starr Calhoun being ID'd in the bank surveillance tape six years ago. Also the lesser story about her older brother Lubbock Calhoun being arrested not long after that.

She'd forgotten about where Lubbock had been arrested, though. It wasn't until she'd been looking for a job away from Fort Worth that her job search had popped up a newspaper reporter position in Whitehorse, Montana, on her computer and triggered the memory of Lubbock's arrest.

Too excited to wait until she saw him the next day, she had called her friend Bradley. Bradley Harris worked in fact-checking at the news station. The two had become good friends almost at once. He loved Tex-Mex food and old movies and was safe because he was gay and Andi didn't date men she worked with. Actually she didn't date at all—too busy with her career, she told herself.

"Why Montana? It sounds like a one-horse town," Bradley had joked when she'd told him about the job, leaving out the part about Lubbock being arrested near there. "Surely there is somewhere closer you could disappear to. Wait a minute." He knew her too well. "How close is this town to where Lubbock Calhoun was arrested?"

Bradley was one of the few people who knew about her interest—or obsession as he called it—in the Calhoun crime family. She'd thought he wouldn't make the connection.

Reluctantly she'd showed Bradley on a Montana map on her computer. Lubbock Calhoun had been arrested for an outstanding warrant in a convenience store in Glasgow, Montana, six years ago—an hour away from Whitehorse.

"I think it's a sign I should check into this job," she said and waited for Bradley to talk her out of it.

And Bradley had tried, pointing out that it had been six years, Lubbock was probably just passing through Montana, and "What could you possibly learn after all this time? Not to mention, you'll be stuck in One Horse."

"Whitehorse," she'd corrected, the job having taken on more appeal with the possible Lubbock Calhoun connection.

"I'm worried about you and this thing with the Calhouns," he'd said. She suspected he knew why they held such interest for her because he was the best researcher she'd ever known. But he never let on.

He'd finally given up trying to stop her, knowing how desperately she needed to get out of Fort Worth. And how she couldn't turn down even a remote chance to learn more about the Calhouns.

Coincidence? Starr coming to Montana, marrying a cowboy from Whitehorse and Lubbock being arrested just miles away? No way. Andi felt her excitement building. There was a story here, the kind of story that had propelled Andi's rise in broadcast news. That and her instincts when it came to investigative reporting.

And while she might have had to give up television news for a while, a story like this would definitely assist in her return when the time came.

Eagerly she planned how to proceed. She had to get the whole story and that meant hearing Cade Jackson's side of it, she thought as she looked up his address in the phone book.

As she took it down, she couldn't help but wonder. Did Cade Jackson know who he'd married? Or was he in for the surprise of his life?

CADE JACKSON walked home from the parade through the underpass beneath the tracks as the passenger train pulled in.

The night was cold and dark, the streets snowpacked and icy. He breathed in the air. It felt moist, the clouds low, another snowstorm expected to come in by tomorrow morning.

A white Christmas. He could hear carols coming from one of the cars' radios as it passed. He quickened his step, anxious to get back to his apartment behind the bait shop. Going to the parade had been a mistake. Now he felt antsy. He thought about driving out to his cabin on Nelson Reservoir, but it was late and he was tired.

The parade had brought back memories of Grace and the night they'd come to the parade together, cuddled close as music played on a float with a Western band. She'd looked over at him, her eyes bright with excitement, her cheeks flushed from the cold. And he'd kissed her.

He could still remember the way she'd tasted. Sweet and just a little pepperminty from the candy cane she'd eaten. He recalled the way she felt in his arms and how happy he'd been. Newlyweds. They'd been newlyweds and he'd thought they had years together ahead of them.

That was the night they talked about having children, he realized as he finally reached the bait shop. He started around back to his apartment in the rear when he saw that someone had left a note on the shop's front door.

He stepped over to pluck it free before going around to the back. While he locked the bait shop door, like most everyone in Whitehorse, he left his apartment door open.

Stepping inside, he flipped on a light glad to be distracted from his thoughts as he opened the note. Something fluttered to the floor, but he was busy looking at the note, surprised he didn't recognize the handwriting.

He knew everyone in Whitehorse, having grown up in the area. He and his brother, Carter, had been raised down by Old Town Whitehorse to the south, but they'd both gone to high school here.

The town of Whitehorse had sprung up to the south closer to the Missouri River breaks, but when the railroad had come through in the 1800s, the town had moved north, taking the name with it.

The note read: "Mr. Jackson, I need to talk to you, M. W. Blake." There was a local phone number at the bottom. And four little words that ruined his night. "It's about your wife."

The word "wife" jumped out at him. He glanced down at the floor and saw the business card at his feet. Bending, he stooped to pick it up. This he recognized. The logo was from the *Milk River Examiner,* the local weekly newspaper.

Under it was the name: M. W. Blake

Under that was the word: Reporter

He crumpled both the note and the business card in his fist. He didn't have any idea who M. W. Blake was and he didn't care to know. The last thing he planned to do was talk to a reporter about Grace.

ON THE WAY HOME after leaving a note for Cade Jackson at his bait shop, Andi realized she couldn't wait until morning to find out what was on this cassette tape. She called the publisher and asked if anyone had a tape player that took regular-size cassette tapes.

His daughter just happened to have an old one she

no longer used, he said. If she stopped by, she was welcome to borrow it. He also had a couple of tapes she could use if she needed to tape something.

Mark Sanders had bent over backward since she'd applied for the job. She'd told him she needed a change of pace. He, in turn, had needed a reporter after Glen Whitaker had been murdered. Not a lot of reporters wanted to come to Whitehorse, especially after they found out what it paid.

Sanders had been worried that Andi had too much experience and wouldn't be staying long.

"Whitehorse is nothing like Fort Worth," he'd said with a laugh. "Maybe you'd better come up here and have a look-see before you take my offer." He had already apologized for how little he could pay her.

She'd had to convince him that Whitehorse was exactly what she was looking for. She didn't tell him her real reason. Only her friend Bradley knew that.

Back at her apartment, Andi took the cassette tape from her pocket and popped it into one side of the player. Hitting Play, she turned up the volume and went into the kitchen to pour herself a glass of wine.

At first all she heard was static. She was beginning to think that the tape was blank as she took the wine bottle from the fridge.

But as she reached for a glass, she heard a woman's voice on the tape and froze.

Like a sleepwalker, she moved into the living room, the wine bottle in her hand as the tape continued.

She didn't recognize the voice—she'd never heard

Starr Calhoun speak. Nor did the woman have much of a Texas accent. No, it was what the woman was saying that captured all of Andi's attention and convinced her that the voice was that of Starr Calhoun.

On the tape, the woman talked about robbing a series of banks. After a moment, a male voice could be heard on the tape. Her accomplice.

The tape went to static but Andi didn't move. Couldn't. She stood too shocked to do anything but stare at the tape player.

Who had sent this to her?

And why?

And where had it been the last six years?

She told herself not to look a gift horse in the mouth. Why not just revel in her good luck at having a story like this dropped into her lap?

But she knew that hadn't been the case. It was no coincidence someone had sent her this. Just as it was no coincidence she was here. Was it possible that someone had sent her the job notice, counting on her need to escape Fort Worth and her interest in the Calhouns? With Lubbock's arrest just miles from here the person who'd sent her the job notice knew she wouldn't be able to resist.

Just as she wouldn't be able to resist breaking this story once she had all the facts.

She stepped to the player, her fingers trembling as she rewound the tape and listened to it again before she went to the kitchen and poured herself a healthy glass of wine. She was shaking now, the realization of what she had in her possession starting to sink in along with the apprehension.

She needed to talk to her friend Bradley. He'd been her sounding board through the whole secret-admirer-turned-stalker trauma in Texas. She dialed his number, needing him to be home.

"So how's the weekly newspaper business," Bradley said after they'd exchanged pleasantries about the weather in Montana versus Texas and he'd told her the TV-station gossip.

She hesitated but only for a moment before she told him about the story she'd stumbled across. Bradley, being Bradley and a journalist at heart, was ecstatic.

"What an incredible story," he cried. "So you were right about there being something to Lubbock Calhoun's arrest up there. Well, that's why you're the hotshot news celebrity and I'm the lowly researcher," he joked. "And to have this story dropped in your lap…" He suddenly turned serious. "Oh, sweetie, I almost forgot. I saw on the news that Lubbock Calhoun was released from prison three weeks ago and has already broken his parole."

Her heart leaped to her throat. Lubbock was on the loose?

"You don't think he's the one who sent you the information, do you?" Bradley asked.

"Why would he?" she asked, although she already knew.

"Isn't it obvious? He figures a hotshot reporter like you will find the money," Bradley said.

She bristled at the hotshot reporter comment. "I work for a weekly newspaper."

"Now you do. Stop being so modest. You are a great reporter. Lubbock must have seen you on TV during one of your stories that made national news," Bradley said. "Sweetie, I don't like this. I think you should hightail it back to Texas. If Lubbock Calhoun's feeding you this information, then it's too dangerous. The man is a hardened *criminal*."

"You know I can't come back to Texas."

"But can you stay there? What if I'm right and he's hoping you find the money for him?"

"It would make quite the story," she said, only half joking.

"Sweetie, but what if you don't find the money?"

"For all I know Starr faked her death and has already spent all the money," Andi said and took a drink of her wine, unnerved by the news about Lubbock. "Don't forget Houston. He could have already blown the money. No one has seen him since he and Starr pulled off that last robbery six years ago."

"If Houston *was* her accomplice," Bradley pointed out. "We know it wasn't Lubbock. He didn't resemble the man in the bank surveillance photos. Plus he was arrested on an old warrant so he wasn't even a suspect in the robberies apparently."

Andi had been thinking about the millions of stolen dollars. "You can bet one of the Calhouns has already spent that robbery money."

"If that were the case, wouldn't Lubbock Calhoun

know that—if he's the one who sent you the information?" Bradley asked.

He made a good point.

"Maybe he doesn't know what happened to the money—or Starr or Houston. Maybe he's winging it just like me," she said.

"Maybe. Or maybe Starr hid the money, planning to take off with her new identity, but hadn't planned on losing control of her car and dying."

"That's another possibility," she admitted. "That's the problem. There are too many possibilities."

"Oh, wait," Bradley said, "but if Starr had hidden the money, surely her husband would have found it by now. Unless he *did* find it!"

"Is there some way to find out if any of the stolen money ever turned up?" she asked.

"The robberies were during the day, right? Banks have what they call 'bait' money. It's traceable. So if any of it has surfaced… I'll see what I can find out and get back to you," he said, sounding as excited as she felt about the story.

She gave him her new cell phone number and they both promised to keep in touch.

After she hung up, she shot a glance at her front window as a car drove slowly by. Lubbock wasn't just out of prison, he'd already broken parole.

Quickly she stepped to the window and closed the curtains, telling herself that the smartest thing she could do was to take everything she knew to the local sheriff, Carter Jackson, Cade Jackson's brother.

But then the story would break prematurely. A story that belonged to her. And not the whole story. Not to mention that she might never find out who was sending her the information or what they wanted.

She checked to make sure her door was locked before she rewound the tape and listened to it again, her mind racing. She took one of the blank tapes Mark Sanders had given her and put it in the second cassette deck and made a copy of the original.

Wouldn't anyone who wanted the story to come out have gone to the sheriff? Or the FBI? Or if not that, a major television station?

Whoever had given her the newspaper clipping and the tape wasn't after a story—or justice. No, they wanted something else. Bradley had to be right. They wanted the money.

She took the tape out of the player and stared down at it. The big question was what was *she* going to do with this?

Chapter Three

The Jackson Bait Shop was on the edge of town. The sign was weathered, the building small. As Andi got out of her car the next morning, she wondered how Cade Jackson made a living in such a remote place selling bait.

Or was he living off the three million dollars Starr had stolen?

Andi had gone into the newspaper early, gathering everything she could find on Cade Jackson. There hadn't been much. A local cowboy, he'd grown up on a ranch south of here near what was called Old Town Whitehorse.

Since then he'd won some horse-roping events and caught a few big fish that had made the newspaper.

His only claim to fame just might turn out to be marrying Starr Calhoun, she thought as she saw that the Closed sign was still up in the bait shop window. There were no store hours posted. Did anyone even fish this time of year?

She knocked at the door and waited on the small landing out front, hugging herself, trying to keep warm.

She guessed he was already up since the *Great Falls Tribune* newspaper box next to the door was empty. It had snowed again last night, coating the entire town with a couple of inches. The snow glittered so bright it was blinding. But it was the breeze that cut through her, chilling her to the bone. She'd had no idea it would be this cold up here.

As a gust of wind whirled snow around her, she instinctively reached for the doorknob. To her surprise, it turned easily in her hand, the door falling open.

She was hit with a blast of warm air. She leaned into it, stepping into the room and closing the door behind her as she tried to shake off her earlier chill.

Apparently Cade Jackson sold more than bait. The room was divided into four long aisles by three high shelves filled with lures and jigs, rods and reels, paddles and oars, nets and an array of boat parts and sporting equipment.

Cade Jackson was nowhere in sight but she thought she heard water running somewhere in the back.

She moved through the shop toward the sound. It was warm in here and she was in no hurry to go back outside into the cold.

But she reminded herself: for all she knew this man had known about the robbery, might even have gotten rid of his wife to keep all the money for himself.

But if he had the three million dollars or even some of it, he didn't appear to be enjoying it much, she thought as she saw his living quarters.

The shop opened onto a small apartment. The lack

of stuff made her wonder if anyone could live this simply. Certainly not Starr Calhoun.

For a moment Andi considered what she was doing. This felt all wrong. Not to mention she couldn't guess what Cade Jackson's reaction was going to be to not only her being here, but also what she had to show him.

What if she was wrong?

She wasn't and she knew it.

But she still felt apprehensive. She had no idea what this man was like. The fact that Starr Calhoun had married him was a clue, though. Andi was wondering if she'd made a mistake coming here alone.

She was no fool, though. In her large shoulder bag, along with a copy of the cassette she'd made and the boom box, she had a can of pepper spray and her cell phone.

"Mr. Jackson?" she called from the doorway into the apartment. No answer.

She called his name again. The sound of running water stopped. "Hello!" she called out. "Hello?" She stopped to look at a bulletin board filled with photographs of fish being held by men, women and children. Some of the fish were as huge as the grins on the many faces.

When she looked up, she was startled to find the apartment doorway filled with a dark silhouette. She got the impression Cade Jackson had been standing in the doorway for some time studying her.

To make things even more awkward, his dark hair was wet and droplets of water beaded on his lashes as well as on the dark curls of his chest hair that formed a V to disappear into the towel wrapped around his slim hips.

"I'm sorry, the door was open," she said quickly.

He smiled either at the fact that he had her flustered or because of her accent. "The shop isn't open yet, but then again you don't look like a fisherman," he said eyeing her. "Nor do you sound local."

"No, I'm neither," she said, getting her composure back. He was even more handsome up close and personal.

He cocked a dark brow at her.

"I'm Miranda Blake. I left my business card and a note on your door last night? But I can wait while you dress."

He'd looked friendly before. He didn't now. "M. W. Blake, the new reporter over at the *Examiner?*" He was shaking his head and moving toward her, clearly planning to show her out. "I don't talk to reporters."

"You'll want to talk to *me*," she said standing her ground as she put her hand on her shoulder bag, easing the top open so she could get to her pepper spray.

He stopped in front of her and she caught a whiff of his soap. Yum. He stood a good head taller. She had to tilt her face up to look into his eyes. Eyes so dark they appeared black. Right now they were filled with impatience and irritation.

"I'm afraid you're mistaken about that, Tex."

"I have some information about your wife," she said, determined not to let him intimidate her but it was difficult. The look in his eyes alone would frighten someone much larger than herself. She clutched the pepper spray can in her purse.

He was as big a man as she'd first thought, a few inches over six feet and broad at the shoulders. Solid looking, she thought. Not like a man who worked out. More like a man who worked. That surprised her given that selling bait and tackle couldn't be all that strenuous.

He settled those dark eyes on her. Everything about him was dark. She tried to imagine someone like Starr Calhoun with this man. Starr with her wild, curly auburn hair and those pale blue eyes, as fair as this man was dark.

"You're new here," Cade Jackson said as if roping in his irritation. "You don't know me. So I'm going to cut you some slack. I don't want another story about my wife's death. It's Christmas and I don't need any more reminders that she's gone, all right?"

"I think you'd better look at this," she said, slipping her hand from the pepper spray can to the copy of the photo taken from the bank's surveillance camera. It had gone out to all news media six years ago, but she doubted it had made it as far as Whitehorse, Montana.

Cade didn't take the photo she held out. He stood with his hands on his hips, dripping on the wood floor of the bait shop, the white towel barely wrapped around his hips showing way too much skin.

"Please. Just take a look and then I promise to leave," she said.

With obvious reluctance he took the copy of the photograph. She watched his expressive dark eyes. Recognition then confusion flashed in them. "What the hell is this?"

"It's your wife. Only her name wasn't Grace Browning. It was Starr Calhoun. That photo was taken by a surveillance camera in the bank she robbed six years ago—not long before she showed up here in White-horse."

"Get out," he said. "I don't know what your game is, Tex, but I'm not playing."

"Neither am I," she said as he reached for her arm. "Starr Calhoun was one of the infamous bank-robbing Calhouns from Texas," she said, dodging his grasp, her hand again clutching the can of pepper spray in her purse. "The three million dollars she and her male accomplice stole was never recovered."

"If you don't get out of here right now, you're going to be sorry," he said through gritted teeth. "What the hell do you keep reaching in that purse for?" He grabbed her arm.

As he jerked her hand out of the shoulder bag, her finger hit the trigger on the pepper spray.

ON THE LAPTOP propped up in her kitchen, Arlene Evans studied the latest applicant on her Meet-A-Mate site with pride as she whipped up a batch of pancakes.

Since she'd started her rural online dating service she'd had a few good-looking men sign up but none who could match Jud Corbett, a former stuntman and actor, who liked long walks in the rain, horseback riding, dancing in the moonlight and was interested in finding a nice cowgirl to ride off into the sunset with.

Arlene had proven she was a great matchmaker when she'd gotten the Whitehorse deputy sheriff together with that Cavanaugh girl.

But that was nothing compared to who she had picked out for the handsome Jud Corbett.

Her very own daughter Charlotte. True, Charlotte wasn't a cowgirl, so to speak, but she could ride a horse. And Jud Corbett was just what her daughter needed right now.

Charlotte had seemed a little down lately. But a man like Jud Corbett could bring her out of it quick!

The two would make beautiful children together, Arlene thought with longing as she broke a couple of eggs into the batter and stirred as she admired Jud Corbett's good looks. If she were twenty years younger…

"Are the pancakes about ready?" her son Bo demanded. At twenty-one, Bo had gotten his looks and personality from his father, damn Floyd Evans to hell.

Floyd had up and left them a few months ago. The divorce papers were somewhere on the overflowing coffee table. The bastard had left her with their three children to finish raising.

Not that the three weren't pretty much raised since the oldest, Violet, was in her thirties, unmarried and no longer under the roof, but that was another story. Bo was of legal age, although that didn't seem to mean anything other than he drank beer in front of her now. Charlotte had just celebrated her eighteenth birthday, eating most of the cake all by herself before going out with her friends and getting high.

The phone rang before Arlene could come up with a proper retort for her son. It rang another time but neither of her offspring seemed to hear it.

"Let me get that, why don't you?" Arlene said

doubting they got her sarcasm, either, since neither seemed to hear anything over the blaring television.

"Mrs. Evans?" a woman said on the other end of the line.

Arlene didn't correct her. "I'm not buying anything," she snapped and started to hang up the phone.

"I'm calling about your daughter Violet."

Arlene put the receiver back to her ear. "Yes?" she asked suspiciously. Calls about Violet were never good.

"My name is Myrna Lynch, I'm the media coordinator here at the state hospital. Your daughter Violet would like you all to come up for Family Day."

"*Family* Day?" Arlene Evans echoed into the phone. "You can't be talking about my daughter. Violet is completely out of it and the last time I came up there to see her you guys wouldn't even let me in."

Arlene was still mad about that. As if she enjoyed driving clear up to the state mental hospital to be turned away.

"No one told you?" asked the woman whose name Arlene couldn't remember. "Your daughter Violet has made remarkable progress. She's no longer in a catatonic state."

"What are you saying? She's not nuts anymore?" How was that possible? "Did she tell you what she did to end up there?"

"Mental illness is a medical disorder that is treatable, Mrs. Evans. Your daughter is getting care that will let her be a responsible member of society again," the woman said, clearly upset at Arlene's use of the word "nuts." "In order to do that, she needs to work through any issues she has with her family. So can I tell the doctor you and your family will be here Saturday?"

"Wait a minute. Issues? She tried to kill me!" Arlene bellowed.

"Your daughter doesn't recall any of that, Mrs. Evans."

Arlene just bet she didn't.

"Violet needs the support of her family. I'm sure you want to do what is best for her."

Arlene bristled at the woman's tone. "I've always supported Violet. You have no idea what I have done for that girl and what did I get for it? Why she—"

"Mrs. Evans, if you can't attend family day Saturday then—"

"I'll be there," she said with a sigh.

"Violet has asked that her brother and sister also attend," the woman said.

Arlene glanced over at her daughter Charlotte curled up on the couch chewing on the end of her long blond hair. Bo was slouched in the recliner, a jumbo bag of corn chips open on his lap and an open can of beer at his elbow, in his own catatonic state as he stared at some reality show on the television where a woman was shrieking at one of the other contestants.

"Turn down the damned TV," Arlene yelled, covering the mouthpiece. "Can't you see I'm on the phone?"

Neither of her grown children responded.

"I have to bring Charlotte and Bo?" Arlene asked the woman, turning her back to the two. "I'm not sure it's a good idea for them to be around Violet."

"It's important for *Violet's* healing process."

"Well, whatever is important for Violet," Arlene snapped. "Never mind the rest of us. She really is better?"

"I think you will be surprised when you see her. We'll plan on your family Saturday."

Arlene hung up, wondering how Violet could surprise her more than she had. Her old-maid daughter had plotted to kill her and even gotten her brother and sister involved.

Arlene could never forgive Violet for that. She'd been so sure her daughter would never get out of the mental hospital and now this. *Family* Day.

Surely those fools at that hospital weren't really considering letting Violet out?

As she spooned the pancake batter into the smoking skillet, the scent of oil and sizzling pancake batter filled the kitchen and adjoining living room.

Behind her, Charlotte made an odd sound, then sprung up from the couch to run down the hall, her hand over her mouth. It was the fastest Arlene had seen the girl move in years. A moment later she heard Charlotte retching in the bathroom.

"What on earth is wrong with her?" Arlene demanded of her son.

He glanced away from the TV to scowl at his mother. "What do you think? She's pregnant. Haven't you noticed how big she's been getting? Where have you been?" He looked past her and swore. "Damn it, Mother, you're burning the pancakes!"

CADE JACKSON swore as he wrenched the can of pepper spray from Andi.

Unfortunately the spray nozzle had been pointed in the wrong direction—her direction. Fortunately only a little had shot out. Enough that her eyes instantly watered and she began to cough uncontrollably.

He grabbed her, cursing with each step as he tried to drag her to the back of his apartment. She fought him, although it was clearly a losing battle, unaware of what he was trying to do until he shoved her out the back door and into the fresh air.

She took huge gulps, tears running down her face as she coughed and tried to get the fresh air into her lungs.

He stood for a moment shaking his head, his arms crossed over his bare chest, his dark eyes boring into her.

"I think you're going to live," he said, giving her can of pepper spray a heave. It landed in the deep snow out by the trees along the Milk River and disappeared. "Now get the hell off my porch."

He stepped back inside, not even looking chilled though still only wearing a towel, and slammed the door behind him. She heard the lock turn.

ON THE OTHER SIDE of the door, Cade Jackson took a ragged breath and looked down at the grainy photograph still clutched in his hand.

It wasn't Grace. True it looked enough like her to be her twin. Enough like her to rattle the hell out of him.

The woman in the photograph, Starr Calhoun, had

robbed a bunch of banks and gotten away with three million dollars?

He wanted to laugh. Not for a minute would anyone believe that this Starr Calhoun was Grace except some wet-behind-the-ears reporter. It was beyond crazy.

He realized he was shaking. From anger. From shock. From the scare she'd given him. Earlier, for just a fleeting panicked instant, he'd thought the woman in the photo was Grace.

It was clear why the reporter had thought so as well as he took one last look at the photo. Even the poor quality print revealed a little of Grace in this woman and it shook him to his core. It was the eyes. She had Grace's eyes.

The reporter had made an honest mistake, he told himself as he balled up the photo of Starr Calhoun and tossed it in the trash can. The rumpled-up photograph landed on the note and business card the reporter had left the night before. M. W. Blake. He still wanted to break her pretty little neck for giving him such a scare. And that stunt with the pepper spray…

He shook his head as he returned to his apartment at the back of shop to get dressed. Someday he would look back on this and laugh. Let Tex wait by the phone. He wouldn't be calling her.

Still he felt shaken by the encounter. Anyone would have been rattled, though, he told himself, after being caught coming out of his shower first thing in the morning by someone like Ms. Blake. He'd foolishly left the shop's front door open after getting his newspaper this morning. Maybe he'd better start locking his apartment, as well.

When he'd first seen her standing there, he'd been a little surprised but he sure hadn't expected what was coming. Not from someone who looked like her, small, demure, sweet looking and sounding with that Texas accent of hers. And a determination that rivaled his own.

Too bad he couldn't shake off the worry that pressed on his chest like a two-ton truck. The woman wasn't foolish enough to run the story, was she?

As he started to leave, he went back into the shop to retrieve the photo, note and business card from the trash. Smoothing the photo, he felt his original jolt of surprise. He quickly folded the paper and stuck all three items in his coat pocket as he headed for the door again.

Cade would just show the photo to Carter, have him find out who this Starr Calhoun was and put an end to this foolishness before the reporter made a fool of herself and tarnished Grace's memory. That, after all, was the benefit of having a brother who was sheriff.

Cade glanced at his watch, knowing where to find his brother this time of the morning. At the same place he was seven days a week, the Hi-Line Café.

Leaving his Closed sign in the window, Cade headed for the café just a few blocks to the west. It was one of those beautiful December days, cold and crisp, the sky a crystalline-blue, the clouds mere wisps high above him and the new snow brilliant and blinding.

It was supposed to snow again by evening, he'd heard on the radio this morning before his shower. The shower brought back the image of M. W. Blake standing in his bait shop. He remembered now that his first impression had been one of male interest—before he'd found out who she was and what she wanted.

He recalled being a little taken aback by the sharp pang of desire he'd felt. But given how long it had been, he supposed he shouldn't have been surprised. The feeling had been more than lust, though. He'd actually been interested.

Even before she'd opened her mouth, it had been clear she wasn't local. She was wearing some fancy black boots with a gray pin-striped three-piece suit and a lightweight leather coat, her long dark hair pulled up to give him a good view of her long, graceful neck.

When she'd turned, he'd been thrown off guard by how young she was. It was the freckles she'd failed to completely hide with makeup and those wide green eyes. Wisps of dark hair curled on each side of the high cheekbones. She was a stunner. The soft Southern drawl was just icing on the cake.

He swore under his breath. She wasn't even half as appealing when it turned out she was a damned reporter, though. And it had only gotten worse when he realized she was a reporter who didn't have her facts straight. What could he expect of someone who was obviously too young to be anything but a rookie?

As he passed the big bare-limbed cottonwoods along the Milk River etching dark against the bright day, he thought of the fall day he'd met Grace and felt a sharp jab of longing.

The woman in the photo hadn't been Grace, but even

the resemblance to her made him hurt all over again. He cursed the damned reporter all the way to the café.

Sheriff Carter Jackson was sitting at the counter. Cade dropped onto the stool next to him and motioned to the waitress that he would have the same thing he always did. Coffee.

"Good mornin'," he said to his brother as the waitress slid a cup in front of him.

"Is it?" the sheriff said.

The waitress brought Cade extra sugar packets. He tore open a half dozen and poured them into his cup.

"If you don't like coffee, why drink it?" Carter asked irritably.

"Who says I don't like coffee?" He poured in most of the small pitcher of milk the waitress brought and glanced at his brother, wondering what had put Carter in such a foul mood. He suspected he knew. Eve Bailey.

Carter had been trying to get Eve back for months now. They'd dated in high school but Carter had married someone else. Now divorced, he wasn't finding Eve Bailey very forgiving. Not that Cade could blame her, although it was clear his brother had always loved her.

"You're up early," Carter said, eyeing him. "What's goin' on with you?"

Cade had planned to show his brother the photo of Starr Calhoun and tell him about the ridiculous claim made by the new reporter in town. But something stopped him.

"Nothin'," Cade said. "Just thought I'd join you for a cup of coffee this morning."

His brother turned now to stare at him. "You sure you're all right?"

"Don't I look all right?" Cade shot back.

"You look a little peaked."

Cade concentrated on his coffee, telling himself he was a fool not to show his brother the Wanted poster and put an end to this. So what was holding him back?

"You're usually out in your ice-fishing house by now," Carter said, sounding suspicious. That also went with having a sheriff for a brother.

"I haven't got my house out yet," he said, although that had been his plan just this morning. Before his early visit from Tex. Normally as soon as Nelson Reservoir froze over he would be on the ice.

"I heard Harvey Alderson speared a nice Northern the other day," Carter said.

Cade nodded. "The photo's already on the wall at the shop." Harvey had come straight there to have his photograph taken. It was a Whitehorse tradition.

"Maybe you're starting to realize there is more to life than fishing," his brother said, sounding as if he thought that was progress.

On any other day Cade might have argued the point. "So how is Eve?"

"She's impossible as ever," Carter groused. "And I don't want to talk about her."

Cade laughed as he watched his brother wolf down his breakfast and between bites, go on and on about Eve. Some things didn't change and today Cade was damned glad of it.

ANDI FINISHED her story on the Parade of Lights and laid out the page for the next day's edition, trying to keep busy.

She'd expected Cade to call. He hadn't.

Wouldn't a man who'd been given evidence that his wife was a known criminal call? Unless he'd already known and was sitting over in his bait shop planning how to keep her from telling another living soul.

She slammed the drawer on the filing cabinet and cursed mildly under her breath. It was time to use her ace in the hole: the cassette tape.

It was dangerous, but once he heard the voice on the tape, he would confirm that the voice was Starr Calhoun's and she would have the proof she needed. She hoped that faced with even more evidence and his own innocence in all this, he would break down and tell her everything about his relationship with Starr.

Unless of course he wasn't innocent.

Andi couldn't help the rush of excitement she felt at just the thought of playing the copy of the tape she'd made for him. Maybe she should have told him about the tape when she'd shown him the photo.

No, she thought, given how angry he'd been she doubted he would have listened to the tape. He had needed time to calm down, to let it sink in, to realize he couldn't hide from the truth.

Right. But how was she going to get him to listen to the tape if he refused to talk to her again? The man was obviously more stubborn than she had anticipated. She'd been convinced, guilty or innocent, he wouldn't be able to rest until he heard her out. So much for that thought.

She sighed as she sat down and checked her schedule. She didn't have another story to cover for several days. The newspaper would hit the stands in the morning and she would have a whole week before the next edition. She couldn't believe how laid-back weekly newspaper work was compared to broadcast news in a metropolitan city.

But it would work out well for her. She'd need time to mine this story. Time to convince Cade Jackson to talk to her.

That was the problem. To get the story she wanted, she needed Cade's side of it. She needed to know how he and Starr had met, how she'd deceived him into marrying her.

Andi felt a twinge of guilt. Cade hadn't just been furious this morning. He'd seemed stunned. Even though he denied the photo was of his wife, she'd seen his shock. He'd recognized Starr.

What would his reaction be when he heard his wife's voice on the tape, callously planning the bank robberies with her accomplice? Unless, of course, Cade *was* her accomplice.

No, the man caught on the bank surveillance cameras had pale blue eyes. Cade Jackson had dark, expressive eyes. Nor was he built like Starr's accomplice.

If Cade Jackson was involved, then it was from the sidelines. Which didn't mean he hadn't known who his wife really was—or that he didn't know what had happened to the robbery money.

A thought struck her like a bolt out of the blue. How badly *had* Starr deceived him? Hadn't the article in the newspaper about her death said that the car had rolled numerous times before catching fire? Her body had apparently burned beyond recognition.

What if Starr had faked her death just as Andi had first suspected? What if she was somewhere living off that three mil with her accomplice? Then who had been killed in the car wreck?

Mind racing, Andi realized the pieces still didn't fit. Lubbock was out of prison and missing. But whoever had sent her the job information about Whitehorse knew she had information about Lubbock's arrest in Montana. That meant the person knew about her interest in the Calhoun family. Might even know about her connection to the Calhouns.

She groaned, realizing how that was possible. A few years back, she'd driven over to the prison where Amarillo Calhoun had been sentenced. The eldest of the Calhoun children, Amarillo had followed in his parents' footsteps, his life of crime going from bank robbing to murder.

She'd seen him sitting in the glassed-in cubicle. Their eyes had met. He must have recognized her because he told the guard he didn't want to speak with her— backing out on their interview. Her face had been all over the TV news. She'd just broken a big news story. That was right before she'd gotten her newscaster job in Fort Worth.

So it was possible Lubbock knew who she was and why she would jump at digging into this story.

If her friend Bradley was right, then Lubbock was after the missing money. Or Starr *and* the money, if she'd faked her death. Or there was Houston Calhoun, who'd disappeared the same time as Starr.

Clearly if Lubbock had left her the tape and newspaper clipping, he wasn't interested in the truth coming out. And he wasn't the only one, Andi thought. Cade Jackson wouldn't want a story about his wife being Starr Calhoun, the bank robber, hitting the news, either, she thought, remembering the look on his face when he'd recognized the woman on the Wanted poster. If he'd loved his wife as much as he appeared to, what would the truth do to him?

She pushed the thought away. She'd never backed down from a story and wasn't going to now. The best stories rose out of someone's pain. This was one of those stories.

A niggling concern wormed its way into her thoughts, though. Whoever was sending her the information was playing her like a marionette until he got what he wanted. Then what?

Her phone rang, making her jump.

"Hello?"

Silence.

"Hello?" she said again, feeling suddenly spooked. Lubbock?

Then to her relief, Cade said, "It's me." He didn't sound happy about it, though.

She waited, suspecting he was sorry he'd called and might even hang up.

"I need to see you," he said gruffly.

"All right. Do you want me to—"

"I'm right outside."

Chapter Four

Cade watched Miranda Blake come out of the newspaper office. She had to be freezing. The temperature was still hovering around zero. Another snowstorm was expected before evening. And here she was dressed like she was still in Texas.

Didn't she notice that no one dressed up in Montana let alone in Whitehorse? And she had to be kidding in those high-heeled boots that certainly were never intended for walking on ice and snow.

He reached across to open the passenger-side door, shaking his head. What the hell was he thinking? He should have just told her what he had to say on the phone. At least he'd left the pickup running. He'd make this quick.

There was a regal air about her that set his teeth on edge as she climbed in and smoothed her suit skirt. She'd brought along an old-fashioned black boom box. What the hell was that about? He turned up the heat, furious with himself for doing this. Why hadn't he left well enough alone?

Because he knew M. W. Blake sure as hell wasn't going to.

"I just wanted to tell you that you're wrong," he said, looking out at the snowy day through the windshield. He'd just have his say then get on his way. "That woman in the photo isn't Grace. Admittedly it resembles her. It sure sent me for a loop." He cleared his throat. "But if you'd known her, you'd know that she wasn't some bank robber and you would have realized your mistake."

She didn't say anything and he was finally forced to look over at her.

"It was an honest mistake, I'm sure," he said. "I just didn't want you doing a story and having to retract it. Nor am I looking for an apology."

She laughed softly. "Well, that's good because I wasn't going to give you one. You're the one who's mistaken."

He jerked off his Stetson and raked a hand through his hair. This woman was impossible. "I'm telling you that photo isn't of Grace."

"No, it's of Starr Calhoun, the woman you married," she said in that sweet southern drawl of hers.

He slapped his hat back on his head and gave the pickup a little gas as he gripped the wheel to keep from strangling the damned woman. "I don't know why I bothered to come by and try to talk sense into you, Tex."

The inside of the pickup cab was warm and smelled of the soap he'd used that morning in the shower. Andi recognized the pleasant scent. "My name is Miranda and you came by to see me because you recognized her and whether you want to admit it or not, you want to know the truth about the woman you knew as Grace Browning."

"Like hell, Tex," he snapped.

As intimidating as he was, she turned to face him. "You can't keep me from doing the story."

"Maybe I can't keep you from making a fool of yourself, but I can sure as hell keep you from involving me in it." He shifted the pickup into gear and gave her a pointed look. "You and I don't have any more to say to each other."

"You're wrong about that. You *are* involved," she said calmly as he reached across and opened her door. A blast of freezing air rushed in.

"Maybe, but you'll have to do your story without my help," he snapped.

"Then I guess you'll have to hear the truth with the rest of the town when it comes out in my article." She started to get out. "Oh, by the way, you should know I'm not the only one who knows about your wife's true identity. Someone sent me a newspaper clipping about her death along with a cassette tape of Starr Calhoun and her male accomplice planning the bank robberies. Want to make a bet it's your wife's voice on the tape?"

He swore and looked away for a moment before he said, "When were you going to tell me about the tape?" He sounded scared and she felt again that prickle of guilt that she was about to destroy this man's life.

"When I thought you could handle it."

He cut his eyes to her, his expression one of anger and fear. He let out a humorless laugh. "And you think I can handle it *now?*"

CADE TOLD HIMSELF that the tape would prove this woman was wrong and that would be the end of it. Not that he didn't realize she was banking on the tape proving just the opposite.

"Fine, let's hear the tape," he said, and reached across her to slam her door.

"I think the sound quality would be better without your pickup truck's engine running in the background, don't you? Also the player's batteries are low. I need to plug it in."

He didn't really want to take her back to his apartment behind the bait shop, but he had little choice. He much preferred doing this on his own turf. And the newspaper office was out. Anyone could come walking in. He sure as hell didn't want an audience.

Pulling out, he flipped a U-turn in the middle of the main street and headed back toward the bait shop.

One of the benefits of living in Whitehorse was the lack of traffic. But today he would have loved a traffic jam. Anything to postpone this.

It wasn't that he feared the voice would be Grace's. All this talk of Grace had brought back the pain. He just wanted to hide as he'd done the last six holidays. He didn't need to see more photographs of women who reminded him of Grace. Or hear some woman's voice that might sound even a little like his dead wife's.

But clearly Miranda Blake wasn't going to give him any peace. Not until he proved her wrong. He glanced over at her, worried about her apparent calm. Did she know something he didn't?

"PREGNANT?" Arlene Evans cried as she threw the spatula at her son.

"Why are you yelling at me? Charlotte's the one who got knocked up, not me," he said and picked up the remote to turn up the sound on the TV.

Arlene grabbed the skillet, tossing the burned pancakes in the trash and turning off the burner before she wiped off her hands and stormed down the hallway.

She wished she was Catholic because she had the strongest urge to cross herself. First Violet and that disgrace and now Charlotte? She couldn't bear it.

Tapping lightly at the bathroom door, she said, "Charlotte, precious, can I come in?"

"No!" Then more retching and the *whoosh* of the toilet as it flushed.

"Open this damned door now or I will break it down," Arlene yelled.

The door opened slowly and Charlotte's bloated face appeared.

Arlene had seen her daughter getting heavier by the day and had just assumed it was all the sweets the girl put away. Violet had always had a weight problem and Arlene hadn't known how to deal with it. She'd told herself that Charlotte, who'd always been slim, would outgrow it.

"What do you want?" Charlotte asked irritably.

Arlene pushed open the bathroom door and stepped in, closing it behind her. She spoke carefully, determined not to lose her temper. "Aren't you feeling well?"

Her daughter gave her a withering look.

"Your brother seems to think you're pregnant but how is that possible?"

Another withering look. Arlene fought the urge to smack the look off her youngest daughter's face.

"You're pregnant?" Her voice broke. One daughter in the nuthouse and one pregnant out of wedlock. She'd never be able to hold her head up in this county again.

Charlotte didn't answer, just looked down at her stomach as she smoothed her large sweatshirt over her protruding stomach.

Arlene was stunned. "Good heavens, how far along are you?"

Her daughter shrugged. "Four months, I think."

Arlene stumbled over to the toilet, dropped the lid and sat. "*Four* months? Four *months* and you don't say a word? What were you thinking?"

Charlotte was still looking down at her stomach as if admiring it.

"Who is the father? Tell me who he is and the two of you can run down to Vegas. No one has to know you didn't get married four months ago."

"I'm not getting married."

Arlene stared at her daughter. Lately Charlotte had been reminding her more and more of Violet, an unpleasant similarity at best. "Of course you're getting married."

Charlotte raised her gaze. "Not likely since he's already married," she said with a chuckle.

Arlene thought she'd have a stroke and imagined the paramedics hauling her out of the bathroom on a stretcher. As if her life wasn't already humiliating enough.

She willed herself not to have a stroke. "Who is he?" She would castrate him. Then kill him.

Charlotte shook her head. "I'm not telling you. I'm never telling you." She gave Arlene a challenging look. "And there is nothing you can do to make me tell."

THE CLOSED SIGN was still in the front window of Jackson's Bait Shop and no customers out front waiting, Cade noticed with relief as he pulled around to the back and got out.

The reporter followed him, bringing along that huge shoulder bag of hers and the boom box. He opened the rear door and stepped aside, clenching his jaw as he let her pass. Now that he was here, he just wanted this over with—and as quickly as possible.

"I don't have a lot of time," he said.

She smiled at that no doubt noticing that there hadn't been a crowd of fishermen beating down his door this morning. But she walked right to his kitchen table and set down the boom box.

He wondered if she had retrieved the can of pepper spray from the snowbank out back or bought more as he watched her plug in the boom box and then produce a tape from her pocket. She dropped the cassette tape into the player and lifted a brow in his direction.

He sighed and stepped over to the table to pull out a chair. Swinging it around, he straddled it and sat down, resting his arms on the back as he gave her an impatient nod. "Let's get this over with."

She hit Play.

At first all he heard was static. The sound was like scraping a fingernail down a blackboard and he flinched, his nerves on edge. He tried to find calm, to breathe. This would be over soon. And yet his heart thudded in his chest with an apprehension that scared him as much as the impossible thought he could have been wrong about Grace.

The static and whir of the tape stopped abruptly with the sound of a female voice.

His heart stopped as well, as he heard a voice from the grave. He tried to catch his breath, his pulse a bass drum in his ears and his limbs numb with a bone-aching chill that rattled through him.

The woman across from him hadn't missed his reaction. Hell, she'd been expecting it. His blood ran colder than the Milk River outside his door and he thought for a moment that he might black out.

There was no doubt about it. The voice on the tape was Grace's. Staggered, he hadn't even heard what she was saying. But slowly, the words began to register.

And just when he thought it couldn't get any worse, he heard another voice, this one male, as the two planned what banks they would rob and in what order.

There was no denying it. The woman he'd married six years ago and lost wasn't who he thought she was.

He stood, knocking over the chair as he lunged at the table to shut off the tape player.

"There's more that you might want to hear," the reporter said.

"Not now." His voice felt as rough as it sounded. "Please go. I need to be alone."

She started to collect the big black tape player.

"Leave it. I'll make sure you get it back."

Her gaze locked with his. "I made a copy of the tape."

"I was sure you had."

She seemed to hesitate, but then rose slowly, all the time watching him as if worried he might come unglued on her.

"I'm fine," he said a little sharper than he'd meant to.

She nodded but didn't look convinced. He figured he probably looked as horrible as he felt.

"Call me when you're ready to talk."

He walked over to the door, opened it and stood waiting, not looking at her. He was afraid of what he'd do if she didn't leave soon.

"Take my truck," he said, removing the keys from his pocket and holding them out to her.

"It's not far, I'll walk."

"Suit yourself."

She stepped out and he slammed the door, leaning against it as he fought to breathe. Grace. Her memory blurred in his mind and he knew even if he pretended this had never happened, Grace Browning was lost to him. More lost than she'd been even in death.

He lurched forward, slamming into the bathroom to be sick.

THERE WAS NOTHING Arlene Evans enjoyed more than a mission. Finding the father of Charlotte's baby was now at the top of her list.

"Take a shower, you smell," she told her daughter as she left the bathroom and walked down the hall.

The television was so loud it made the old windows in the farmhouse rattle. Arlene walked calmly over to where her son slouched in the chair. She picked up the remote and pressed Off.

"What the hell?" Bo demanded, sitting up.

She shoved him back down, snatching the bag of chips off his lap and carefully folding the top down before she put the bag aside. "Who is the father of that baby?"

"You're asking *me?* Why don't you ask her?"

Arlene wet her lips. She liked to think of herself as one of those patient mothers.

"I'm asking you, Bo. Now please tell me. Who has she been with?" Arlene tried again calmly.

"Who hasn't she been with?" he said with a laugh.

Arlene hadn't meant to smack him. If she had, she would have cuffed him harder.

He recoiled, looking hurt and angry, even though she'd barely touched him.

"She said the man is *married.*"

"So?"

"I would think that would narrow the field some," Arlene snapped. "Now think. You're going to help me with this."

Bo groaned and reached for the chips.

Arlene held them out of his reach. "I'm going to make you some pancakes and when I'm done, I expect some names."

ANDI WALKED BACK to her office, the frigid winter air like a slap in the face. The snowstorm moved in before she'd traveled a block. She welcomed it. She was still shaken by Cade's reaction to the voice on the tape—even though she'd known it had to be the woman he'd known as Grace Browning.

The look on his face, the shocked horror, the devastation. If Andi had wondered how he felt about his wife, she didn't anymore. His stricken face had been filled with pain and anguish. Sticking a knife in his heart might have been less painful.

She shivered from the cold, glad she had only a few blocks to go. The fact that she'd been right—Grace Browning *had* been Starr Calhoun—gave her little satisfaction. She glanced back toward the bait shop, hoping Cade was all right, wishing he wasn't alone, a little afraid of what he might do.

Not that she had any choice but to leave. She'd known better than to argue with him. He'd already thrown her out once today.

Afraid he's going to off himself before you get the rest of the story?

She bristled, hating that he'd been hurt. But he'd needed to hear the truth. It wasn't as if this all wouldn't come out even if she didn't do the story.

Not that this wasn't going to be an amazing story and

it would do even more amazing things for her career. She would get national recognition.

But that really wasn't the point. She wasn't doing this story for her career. This one was personal and she'd see it through till the end—no matter how difficult this was for Cade.

Clearly he hadn't moved on with his life since his wife had died. Once this was over, maybe he finally could.

When Andi looked at it that way, she was doing him a favor.

Nice spin, her irritating conscience noted sarcastically.

"I haven't gotten where I am today by backing down from a story," she snapped, her words lost in a gust of wind and snow.

Yeah, just look where you are.

She told herself that she refused to feel guilty for doing her job and walked a little faster, the earlier chill no longer refreshing.

By the time she reached the newspaper office her teeth were chattering. The air shimmered with snowflakes that whirled around her as if she was inside a snow globe.

She opened the door and hurriedly ducked inside. Immediately she saw that she had the office to herself. Without sitting down at her desk, she pulled out her cell phone and dialed Bradley's number.

"I've been on pins and needles waiting to hear from you," he said without preamble. "Did he hear the tape? What was his reaction?"

"He was devastated," she said, surprised how close

she was to tears. "Until he heard her voice, I don't think he believed she was Starr Calhoun."

"So he really didn't know?"

"No. I just feel so badly for him."

"Let me guess. He's ruggedly handsome."

She shook her head, smiling a little. "He's good-looking, if that's what you're asking, but that has nothing to do with—"

"You feeling sorry for him. Right?"

"He loved her. From what I can gather, he hasn't even dated since she died. Everyone in town who I've mentioned his name to has told me he became a recluse after he lost her."

"So you have a great story," Bradley said.

"Yeah, I guess."

"Excuse me, that isn't you getting emotionally involved, is it? Miss Hard-Core News Reporter."

"He's a victim of the Calhouns. I can relate."

"Yes, I guess you can. I guess when the story breaks it will be a form of justice for you both then."

She smiled ruefully. She'd always suspected he knew her connection to the Calhouns. His comment confirmed it. "You always know what to say." She spotted Shirley heading back to the office. "I have to go. I'll call you." She snapped off her phone and walked to her desk.

It wasn't until she was taking off her coat that she saw the envelope on her desk. Manila, with her name neatly typed on the front. Nothing else. Just like the last one.

Chapter Five

With Charlotte still refusing to divulge the name of the baby's father and Bo, it turned out, knowing little or nothing about his sister's "friends," Arlene was forced to do her own investigating.

Four months ago her daughter had worked at the Whitehorse nursing home. Arlene realized that she'd been remiss in not visiting one of Old Town Whitehorse's leading citizens. The Cavanaughs were as close to royalty as it came in Old Town, and Pearl Cavanaugh was the queen. A few months ago she'd had a stroke and had gone into the home.

Pearl's husband, Titus, still ran Old Town and Whitehorse and half the county if the truth was known. He did everything from preach at the community church to organize every Old Town event. Arlene had heard that he spent hours at his wife's bedside.

Not prone to jealousy, Arlene still couldn't curb her irritation. How had Pearl gotten a man like that when Arlene had gotten *Floyd?* Life wasn't fair, that was for sure, she thought as she pushed open the door to the nursing home carrying the Christmas cactus she'd bought for Pearl.

Arlene asked directions to Pearl's room. She passed Bertie Cavanaugh who scowled at her as she slinked down the hall. The woman always looked guilty.

As she passed Nina Mae Cross's room, Arlene stopped to say hello to McKenna and Faith Bailey who were visiting their grandmother—not that Nina Mae had a clue who they were. Alzheimer's, Arlene had heard.

"I sent you an e-mail," Arlene told McKenna. "I'm still looking for the perfect man for you."

The cactus was getting heavy so she hurried on down to Pearl's, anxious now to get this over with.

She'd checked out the staff on her way and was disappointed to find that most of the people who worked here were female. The new doctor in town was practically a baby himself—and single. And the one male orderly was anything but her daughter's type.

To Arlene's surprise, Pearl was sitting in a wheelchair by the window. When had she gotten well enough for a wheelchair? She turned as Arlene entered the room.

"Pearl," Arlene said loudly. "How are you?"

"Her hearing is fine," said a male voice behind her.

Arlene turned to find Bridger Duvall standing in the doorway. He moved to Pearl's side. "She can understand you but she's having a little trouble talking, aren't you, Pearl?" He took the elderly woman's hand in both of his and gently stroked the pale skin.

Pearl smiled, a lopsided smile but nonetheless a smile, shocking Arlene.

"I didn't realize you knew Pearl," she said. After all, Bridger Duvall was a mystery. No one really knew who he was or why he'd come here. He'd opened a restaurant in town with Laci Cavanaugh, Pearl's granddaughter.

That, Arlene realized, must explain this odd friendship.

"I brought you a cactus," Arlene said to Pearl, enunciating each word carefully.

"How thoughtful," Bridger said, taking it from Arlene to place the plant over by the window.

"She's certainly doing well." The last Arlene had heard Pearl was paralyzed and unresponsive. Now she looked alert. But then Pearl Cavanaugh had always been a sharp old broad.

"I just stopped by to say hello," Bridger said, returning to Pearl's side. "Laci and I are cooking for parties all month. Not that we're complaining. Business has been good."

Pearl smiled up at him and said something Arlene couldn't understand.

"I'll give Laci your love. She's busy baking Christmas cookies. She'll be bringing some down to the staff. You know how she is."

What could have been a chuckle arose from Pearl.

As Bridger started to leave, Arlene said, "I'll walk out with you." She waved over her shoulder at Pearl. "Glad to see you're doing so well."

Once out in the hall, Arlene said to him, "You

spend a lot of time here? You might know my daughter, Charlotte."

He nodded.

"I was wondering if you've seen her with anyone, you know, a man, romantically, you understand?"

From the look on his face, he understood perfectly. "I'm sorry, but I wouldn't know anything about that. Now if you'll excuse me."

As Arlene watched him hurry away, she looked back at Pearl. The old gal had a sympathetic look on her face. There was nothing Arlene Evans hated worse than pity, she thought, as she hurried down the hall and out into the cold December day.

ANDI STARED at the envelope on her desk for a long moment. Then she put her coat on the back of her chair and, rubbing her freezing hands together, sat down. Like her coat and boots, her gloves were a thin leather that had been perfect for winters in Fort Worth.

Gingerly she picked up the envelope, turning it in her fingers. No return address, of course. No clue as to who might have sent it.

Shirley, the newspaper receptionist/bookkeeper, had stopped outside to talk to a passerby.

The newspaper had little staff, just Shirley and several columnists who stopped by on occasion. The only time the office was busy was when the publisher and his oldest daughter put the paper together the night before it came out.

Shirley was a grandmother who only worked part-time. Most of that time she was next door at the coffee shop. Apparently everyone in town knew where to find her if they needed anything.

With a sigh, Andi took out her letter opener and sliced the envelope open. Inside was another newspaper clipping. Andi unfolded it, flattening it, then turned the clipping over, frowning.

On one side was an article about Kid Curry's last holdup in the Whitehorse area. On the other side was an ad for tractors. What could this possibly have to do with Starr Calhoun or Grace Browning?

Shirley entered with a latte and fry bread from the shop next door. "Oh, if I'd known you were here I would have brought you something." She was tiny with white hair and small brown eyes.

"Thank you, but I'm fine," Andi said.

Shirley saw the article lying on the desk and smiled. "You like our colorful history?" she asked. "Kid Curry and his brothers hung out up here for a while. Had a place to the south."

"Really?" Andi couldn't imagine what that had to do with Starr Calhoun and the missing bank robbery money.

Shirley quickly warmed to her subject. "This area was home to many an outlaw. It was the last lawless part of the state. You might be surprised how wild this town used to be. Why, one of the outlaws' six-guns is on display at the museum. Can't think of his name right now and my fry bread is getting cold, but you should check it out."

"I'll do that," Andi promised.

As Shirley hurried to her desk in the back, Andi dug

out the first envelope she'd received. She compared the type on both. Identical. Sent no doubt by the same person. Both postmarked Whitehorse.

But what was the connection to Kid Curry? Other than they were all outlaws?

A thought struck her and she wondered why she hadn't considered it before. Was it possible Houston was still in Whitehorse? He could have done what Starr did, found someone, gotten married under an alias and was still living here.

Although if Houston was behind this, she had to wonder why he'd waited six years. Lubbock had been in prison until just recently so the timing made more sense.

She told herself that she didn't care who was pulling her strings. All she cared about was the story. But even as she thought it, she knew that eventually she'd find out who was behind the information being fed to her. And what that person wanted from her.

Folding up the newspaper clipping she shoved it back into the envelope and put it with the other one in her drawer.

"Shirley?" Andi called as she reached for her coat. "If anyone wants me, I'll be at the museum learning about Whitehorse's infamous past."

CADE COULDN'T MOVE, couldn't breathe. He dropped into a chair at the table and covered his face with his hands, telling himself this wasn't happening. Not after six years of grieving. Not after he was finally coming to grips with losing Grace.

Too stunned to hear or feel anything, the hammering at the front door of the shop didn't register for a while. Not that he would have opened the door even if he had heard it before the knocking abruptly stopped.

He stared at the tape player but didn't touch the play button. Not after hearing it three more times. Each time he thought the voice wouldn't be Grace's. Each time, he prayed it wouldn't.

Each time it was.

He heard the crunch of snow outside, then the rattle of the knob as someone tried the back door only to find it locked, something nearly unheard of in Whitehorse.

"Cade?"

At the concern he heard in his brother's voice, Cade rose and went to unlock the door.

One glance at Carter's expression and he knew he must look like hell.

"What's wrong? It isn't Dad, is it?"

Cade shook his head. "Everyone's fine."

His brother came in, closing the door behind him. "Everyone's not fine. You were acting weird at breakfast. And now you look like your best friend died. What's going on?" He glanced toward the large black tape player on the table, the worry in his expression deepening.

"I need a favor," Cade said, knowing his brother. Carter would keep after him until he gave him at least a plausible explanation.

"Are you in some kind of trouble?"

He shook his head. "A *couple* of favors actually.

There's a new reporter in town from Texas. Her name's Miranda Blake. She goes by M. W. Blake."

"This is about a *woman?*" Carter asked incredulously. He laughed, looking relieved.

"I hate to ask but could you see what you can find out about her?"

Carter was smiling. "You had me scared. You looked so horrible, I thought…" He quit smiling and shook his head. "I thought for sure someone had died."

"There is something else," Cade said. "It's about Grace."

His brother instantly looked worried. "Grace?" He seemed to be holding his breath.

Carter had once asked him what it was about Grace that Cade couldn't forget. "Everything," he'd said. *"Everything."*

"I want to close that chapter on my life," Cade said now, meaning it more than he thought possible.

His brother's relief was palpable. After the first couple of years when Cade couldn't seem to get over Grace's death, Carter had become concerned.

"I'm worried about you," he'd said. "I'm afraid you're never going to get over this."

Cade had smiled ruefully. "I don't think I am."

"In order to move on," Cade said now. "I need to find out if Grace's parents are still alive."

"I thought she said they were dead?" Carter asked in obvious surprise.

"That's what she told me, but I learned something recently that makes me wonder," he said. "Could you see what you can find out? I don't want to contact them, I just want to find out if what Grace told me was true."

"Grace have a middle name?" Carter asked, pulling out his notebook and pen. Cade had known his brother would do anything to get him to move on with his life.

"Eden," Cade said.

His brother looked up. "Eden? Like in Adam and Eve?"

Cade shrugged. "I guess so. Her birthday was July 4, 1974."

"Birthplace?"

"Los Angeles, California."

Carter looked up and frowned. "No kidding? I always thought she was born in the South. I wonder where she picked up the accent?"

"Accent?"

"You never noticed her accent?" Carter laughed. "It only came out when she was upset. Like that time you got thrown from the horse. When we were at the hospital waiting for the doctor to tell us how bad it was, I could really hear her Southern accent." He frowned. "Wait a minute. This new reporter…" He glanced at his notes. "She's from Texas?" He swore. "She's got a Southern accent, too?" He looked at Cade with suspicion.

"She's nothing like Grace," Cade said quickly. "And anyway, Grace didn't have a Southern accent."

Carter raised a brow. "You never noticed it?"

"No." He realized that wasn't quite true. A few times he had picked up an accent, but she'd said her father was in the military and they'd spent some time in Alabama when she was young. He'd noticed after that how she seemed to do everything she could to hide it.

Carter put away his notebook and pen and placed a hand on Cade's shoulder. "Don't worry, bro. I'll find out what I can. You didn't say what you heard that made you think Grace's parents were still alive."

Cade shook his head, hating that he was lying to his brother. But he wasn't ready to talk about this. Maybe he was still holding on to the hope that there had been a Grace Browning. Another woman bedsides Starr Calhoun who looked and sounded just like his wife.

"I saw a couple on CNN," Cade said. "Their name was Browning. They lived in Los Angeles and were about the right ages. I swear they looked enough like Grace that they could have been her parents. It just seemed like too much of a coincidence. I know it's crazy."

He saw that his brother agreed. "Heck, why not check it out? I'll let you know what I find," Carter said as he headed for the door. He stopped and glanced back at Cade. "Does it matter if her parents are still alive or not? I mean, are you sure you want to dig up the past?"

"To me Grace was perfect, you know? But the truth is I sensed that she wasn't telling me something about her past. I guess if I found out that she'd lied about her parents being dead it would make it easier to let go for good," Cade said, knowing his brother would buy this explanation.

Carter nodded. "Speaking of favors… I have one to ask of you."

Cade braced himself. He hoped this wasn't about

Christmas. He wouldn't be having any happy holidays this year.

"The families are getting together Christmas Eve at Northern Lights restaurant," Carter said. The families being the Jacksons and the Baileys.

"Yeah, about that…" Cade said quickly. "I'm probably not going to make that."

Carter looked upset. "Not good enough. Not this year. You have to come."

"Maybe I could drop by—"

"Cade, you've missed Christmas now for six years. You can't this year. It's important. The truth is I need you there."

Cade stared at his brother. "You're going to ask Eve to marry you."

Carter gave an embarrassed laugh. "Am I that transparent? Yeah, I am and I need as much of the family there as I can get. Less chance she'll say no."

"She won't say no. She loves you."

"I mean it, Cade, I need you there. You can bring the reporter if that's what you want."

Cade swore silently. "Naw, that's all right. I'll be there."

"Thanks, I really need the moral support." Carter didn't ask why Cade hadn't wanted to come originally. He'd probably just assumed that it was because of Grace. He had no idea just how true that was.

"So you've bought the ring I assume?" Cade asked.

"Dad gave me Mother's," he said a little sheepishly.

Of course Dad would have given it to Carter, their mother's favorite. "Cool," Cade said. "That's great."

"Dad didn't think you'd mind." Carter stepped to him, surprised Cade by pulling him into a hug. "I've missed you, bro. It's good that you'll be there this Christmas."

Cade felt bad that he'd been a recluse for the past six years. He'd burrowed in with his pain, just wanting to be alone to grieve.

He'd been so much better this year. Until that damned reporter had shown up.

Carter drew back looking a little embarrassed. "Okay. I'll see what I can do about finding Grace's parents." He smiled. "And I'll also check on the new reporter for you. I've heard she's a stunner."

"She is that," Cade agreed. She sure as hell stunned him.

Chapter Six

The Whitehorse Museum was housed in a small building on the edge of town. A couple of elderly ladies were behind the desk as Andi entered.

They greeted her warmly.

"Are you doing a story on our museum?" the shorter of the two asked. "She's the new reporter at the *Examiner,*" the woman informed her coworker who nodded.

Andi couldn't help being amused. So few newcomers moved to Whitehorse that apparently she stood out even before she opened her mouth. The way news traveled in this town, she wondered why they even bothered with a newspaper.

On the way to the museum, she'd driven by the bait shop and seen a sheriff's department patrol car parked out front. That worried her. She had no idea what Cade would do.

Had he called his brother and told him about Starr Calhoun? she wondered as she paid her admission price and wandered through exhibits that chronicled everything from the story of the hundreds of thousands of buffalo that had roamed this prairie to the coming of the railroad and the birth of present day Whitehorse.

She found the outlaw exhibit at the back. Apparently Shirley was right. This part of Montana had remained lawless late into the 1800s. Along with Kid Curry, Whitehorse had seen Butch Cassidy, the Sundance Kid and other less-known outlaws. It had been a place of murder and mayhem. Curry had been the leader of the notorious Wild Bunch, was alleged to have killed ten men, although it was said he'd grown up reading the Bible.

According to the museum exhibit, there'd been Western holdup artists, bank robbers, road agents, killers and railroad thieves.

While interesting, Andi was wondering what something that had happened so long ago had to do with Starr Calhoun when she spotted a name that leaped out at her. It was in the part of the exhibit detailing an outlaw named Long Henry Thompson.

Long Henry was credited with having belonged to the Henry Starr gang out of Texas that robbed everything they could, along with stealing livestock on the Texan-Mexican border. Long Henry, wanted in Texas for these crimes, had allegedly hired on to bring cattle to Montana along with some others from the Starr gang.

Andi had heard of Henry Starr. He was descended from the Starr criminal dynasty that began with Tom "Giant" Starr and his son Sam.

Hadn't she read somewhere that Hodge and Eden Calhoun had named their youngest daughter Starr after the famous Henry Starr criminal family that had operated in Texas during the 1800s?

And now it seemed at least one of the Starr gang had ended up in Whitehorse, Montana, back when this part of the country was known for its outlaw hideouts.

Was this the Calhoun connection to Montana? Is this why Starr had come here—just as some of her namesake had more than a hundred years before? The Texas outlaws had changed their names, she realized, and reinvented themselves.

Just as Starr had done.

Was that why she'd been given the Kid Curry clipping? Was whoever had sent her the clippings just seeing whether or not she would follow up each lead?

That would mean, though, that she was being watched. She glanced toward the large plate-glass windows, but all she could see was the falling snow.

She turned back to the exhibit, studying the black and white photographs of robbers—not unlike the one she had of Starr, she thought as she heard the tap of boot heels behind her and turned to see Cade Jackson.

He glanced at the outlaw exhibit and she caught his surprised—and worried—expression. "We need to talk."

CADE WALKED OUT to his pickup. This woman had knocked him for a loop. And now to find her standing in front of the outlaw exhibit… Idle curiosity? Or something more?

He feared he knew exactly what that more might be. But how had she found out?

Because she was hell-bent on finding out everything there was to know about Grace. And, in turn, him.

If he'd doubted before that the woman meant business, he no longer did. His whole life was about to be opened up and every detail exposed to the media. And he didn't need Miranda Blake to tell him that a story like this would go nationwide.

He was losing his past like a shoreline being washed away by waves. He could feel a little more of it drop out from under him, swept out by the storm.

And Tex was that storm. She'd blown in and now she was causing havoc in his life. Worse, with Grace's.

"How did you know I was here?" she asked, stopping short of his truck as snow fell around her.

"I called the newspaper. Shirley said you were at the museum. Get in."

She crossed her arms over her chest and glared at him, unmoving. "What did you want to talk to me about?" Her dark hair sparkled with ice crystals as snow fell around her.

"You want to talk about this out in the middle of a snowstorm? Go right ahead, Tex. I'll be in the truck." He didn't wait for an answer.

"As I told you before, my name is Miranda. Or Andi. *Not* Tex. Remember?" she snapped as she got in and he started the engine.

Miranda sounded too old. Andi was a little too friendly and he was feeling anything but friendly.

"I saw your expression in there," she said. "What was it about the outlaw exhibit that ties in with Starr?"

He shook his head, not in answer, but in awe. The woman was like a bloodhound on his scent and she was tracking his life with an instinct that scared him.

"Don't even bother to tell me that you don't know what I'm talking about," she said, sounding angry. "You *know* something about all this. You couldn't have lived with Starr and not suspected *something*. Why do you keep fighting me?"

He looked over at her. "Because it's my life you want to destroy for a damned news story and fifteen minutes of fame."

She looked chastened. "I'm sorry. I know how hard this must be on you. But this isn't going away just because you want it to."

"*You're* not going away, you mean," he said, trying to curb the anger he felt the instant he was in her presence.

"Even if I left tomorrow, do you really think whoever fed me the information about Starr is going away, as well?"

He didn't know what to think. Or feel. Other than numb. Just not numb enough.

"There's something you should know. Lubbock Calhoun, Starr's brother, was recently released from prison. Apparently he's broken his parole. No one knows where he is."

Cade shot her a look. "You think he's the one who sent you the tape?"

"Well, if it's him, then he's already in town," she said. "The envelope was postmarked Whitehorse."

Cade swore. Just when he thought things couldn't get any worse. What a fool he'd been to think that this might all blow over. "What does he want?"

"Probably the money. Until the three million is found…" She looked up as he backed out onto the highway and turned north. "Where are we going?" She sounded worried.

"I thought we'd take a ride."

"I put the original cassette tape with a copy of all my notes in a secure place," she said, looking away. "In case I should disappear."

He laughed. "I wasn't planning to kill you, Tex."

She glanced over at him. "I guess neither of us have anything to worry about then."

He wished that were true as he drove north out of town on the wide two-lane. A few locals were trying to get the highway across what was known as the Hi-Line made into a four-lane. They had some crazy idea that it would bring more people to this isolated part of the state.

He wasn't opposed to the idea, he just knew it would never fly—not when he could go for miles and never see another car on the highway.

"Tell me about Starr Calhoun," he said after White-horse disappeared in his rearview mirror.

The question seemed to take her by surprise. "Like what?"

"Everything you know about her."

"Okay." She took a breath and let it out slowly. "She is one of six children born to Hodge and Eden Calhoun."

Eden? Grace had picked her real mother's name for a middle name. He felt sick. There was no doubt about who Grace had been.

"Her parents took all the kids with them when they robbed banks until they were captured and the children were put into foster homes."

Grace had been in a foster home? He couldn't help but feel for her, just as he couldn't help but think of her as Grace even if she really had been Starr Calhoun. "What happened to the kids?"

She shrugged. "They grew up. Some of them made the news as they followed in their parents' footsteps."

"And the parents?"

"Hodge and Eden died in prison a few years apart. Hodge was killed by another inmate. Eden killed herself."

He practically drove off the highway. He remembered how sad Grace had looked when she'd told him that both her parents were deceased. Killed in a plane crash, as he recalled. A lie. On top of the biggest lie of all.

"All of the kids dropped off the radar until one after another all but one turned up on police reports," she was saying. "Amarillo, the oldest, died in prison of hepatitis C. Dallas is doing time in California. Houston has been missing since the robberies six years ago. Worth seems to be the only one who went straight. He was the youngest of the boys so he was probably adopted and his name changed. Lubbock…well, who knows where he is?"

Cade couldn't believe what he was hearing about Starr and her family.

"For all we know, Houston could be living in Whitehorse," she was saying. "Did Starr ever mention her family, her brothers?"

"She told me she was an only child." Another lie. "You know an awful lot about the Calhouns," he said.

She looked out her side window even though there was nothing to see but snow. "I'm a reporter. I do a lot of research."

There was more to it, he thought. He couldn't wait to see what his brother found out about Andi Blake. "That's all you know about Starr?"

"I know she robbed a bunch of banks and disappeared," Andi said bristling. "And now I know where she disappeared to—at least for a while."

"What does that mean?"

"Are you sure she's dead?"

"What?" he snapped. "I buried her. You think she walked away from that car accident?"

"Someone died in that car, but how can you be sure it was your wife?"

"She was wearing the wedding band I bought her." He wished he'd left Tex at the museum.

"Was an autopsy done? Was any DNA taken?"

"You think she faked her death?" he asked incredulously.

"She had three million good reasons to fake her death."

"She had at least one damned good reason not to," he snapped and shook his head, wondering how this could be any more painful. If it hadn't been the middle of winter he might have just dumped Tex off beside the road. Let her find her own way home.

"Grace didn't fake her death," he said, trying to keep his voice down. "I know because…" He took a breath and let it out. "Because she'd gone shopping in Billings for my Christmas present. She called on her way home to tell me she had a surprise for me and couldn't wait to tell me. An early present." He glared over at Andi. "She'd been to a doctor. She was pregnant with our baby."

He took satisfaction in the shock he witnessed on Andi Blake's face before he turned back to his driving and fought to swallow back the gutting pain of the memory. "The woman who died in that car on the way back to Whitehorse was two months pregnant with my child. And yes, I know that for a fact. I got a copy of the results from the doctor after she died."

Andi stared at his granitelike profile for a moment before turning to gaze out at the snow-covered landscape. It suddenly felt colder, definitely more isolated.

Starr had been pregnant. The story just kept getting better and better. All she had to do was keep badgering Cade, keep getting the bits and pieces he was trying so hard to keep from her.

She knew she was treading on thin ice. She'd hurt this man, angered him and feared what he might do if she pushed him too hard. She was ninety-nine percent sure he hadn't known who Grace was. But he had to have suspected something wasn't right.

"I'm sorry," she said. Starr hadn't just married Cade Jackson, but she'd also gotten pregnant with his child? That didn't sound anything like the woman Andi had read about in the police reports. Nor the one planning the robberies on the cassette tape.

Starr Calhoun hadn't been talked into robbing banks. She'd been the ring leader. Even if she was pregnant, it didn't mean she'd died in that car six years ago. There was no way of knowing if Starr Calhoun was dead without doing an exhumation.

But Andi wasn't about to voice that. Especially right now, she thought, looking out at the desolate landscape. She couldn't even be sure where they were let alone where they were headed.

Ahead all she could see was snow. It filled the sky, drifted in the barrow pits, clung to the fence posts on each side of the road and covered the rolling hills for miles.

And it was still falling. Earlier on the radio she'd heard something about a winter storm warning alert— whatever that was.

The women at the museum had told them as they were leaving earlier to bundle up because there was a storm coming. Another foot of snow was expected and temperatures were going to drop. She couldn't imagine it getting any colder.

She saw Cade look in his rearview mirror as they topped a hill. Glancing back she saw nothing but empty highway. As she turned around she felt a little sick. The lack of contrast gave her the feeling that the earth was flat white and that if Cade kept driving, he would drive right off the edge of it.

Cade slowed the pickup and turned off the highway. She caught a glimpse of a sign that read Sleeping Buffalo.

"What was that?" she asked as they passed a mangerlike structure that housed two large rocks. She hoped he was taking her somewhere public. Being alone with him was wearing on her nerves. She didn't like how upset he was.

"It's sleeping buffalo," he said. "During the Ice Age, glaciers carved this country leaving behind a field of large boulders the Native Americans thought looked like buffalo. The buffalo had been scarce. When the Indians saw the two rocks, they thought they were buffalo and rode toward them. Just as they reached the rocks, though, they saw a huge herd of buffalo beyond them. The two buffalo-appearing rocks were then considered sacred, having led the hunters to the buffalo. The rocks are kept so the Native Americans can pay their respects by leaving tobacco on them."

She took that in as they passed a cluster of buildings that according to the sign was Sleeping Buffalo Resort. She recalled something about a shoot-out there a few months ago. If she had any doubt she was in the Wild West, all she had to do was read the old newspaper stories.

Over the next rise, she saw an expanse of ice dotted with a half dozen small fishing huts. "People really don't fish when it's this cold, do they?"

"If cold stopped 'em, nobody in Montana would fish," he said. "And I'd be out of business."

They drove in silence as the snowpacked road narrowed and a few houses gave way to nothing but rolling, snowy hills. Out here there was no hint of the fast-approaching holiday. Just as there was no Christmas tree or any decorations at her apartment. Or at Cade's. No reminder that Christmas was just days away.

"So what's your life story, Tex?" Cade asked. "Let's hear it. Seems only fair since you're so interested in mine."

She ignored the "Tex." "I don't have a story."

He let out a humorless laugh. "We all have a story. Isn't that how your profession works? You prey on our life stories for the amusement and edification of your readers? But *your* life is private?"

She didn't answer, more concerned about where he was taking her.

"Wasn't there some man you left in Texas?" he asked, glancing over at her. He must have seen the answer in her face although he misread it. "That's what I thought. And you give me a hard time for trying to run away from this?"

"You're mistaken."

"Right," he said with a laugh as he slowed to turn on an even narrower road, the deep snow scraping on the undercarriage of the pickup as he busted through drifts, snow flying.

Andi held on for dear life, afraid now of not only where he was taking her, but also what he planned to do when he got there.

"A woman who dresses like you working for a weekly newspaper in Whitehorse, Montana, and you're telling me you're not running away from something?" He had to fight to keep the pickup in the narrow tracks. "Save your breath."

Had he found out about her broadcast news job in

Fort Worth through his brother the sheriff? "This isn't about *me.* But if you must know, I worked for a television station but I wanted a change of pace."

"A change of pace?" He shook his head. "Come on, Tex, you're into this up to your eyeballs. You're the one who got the newspaper clipping and cassette tape. Not me. Don't tell me you haven't wondered: why *you?* I sure have."

She'd wondered all right. "I'm a reporter. Whoever sent me the information knew I would follow it up."

"Lubbock Calhoun, straight from prison, would know that about you?" he asked.

"Or Houston. For all you know he married someone right here in Whitehorse just like his sister did. He could be your neighbor."

Cade shook his head. "I know all my neighbors and have for many years. Any other theories?"

"I don't know who is sending me the information. I'm sure they have their reasons. If it's Lubbock, then he must have seen me on the news."

"You made the news?"

"I was a TV broadcast newswoman."

"Oh, you *read* the news," he said.

"I did more than *read* the news. I—" She stopped abruptly as she saw the trap he'd laid for her.

"Yes?" he asked smiling over at her. "What? You want your life to remain private? You just tell the news. Forget that it's my life and Grace's memory that you're trying to destroy."

"There was no Grace," she snapped.

"Like hell there wasn't," he shot back. "She was Grace when I fell in love with her, when I married her, when I buried her."

Andi heard the horrible pain in his voice and was hit with a wave of guilt that angered her. She didn't start this. The Calhouns did. She was just doing her job. She was sick of him trying to blame her because his wife was a liar and a criminal.

"You might never have known the truth if I had just ignored it," she snarled.

"Yeah, and wouldn't that have been terrible?" he said sarcastically as he glared over at her for a moment.

"You can't just stick your head in the sand and pretend none of this happened. Whoever is sending me the information about Starr, you think that person is going to keep quiet?"

Cade realized where he was headed and swore under his breath. He hadn't really planned to come out here. Hell, he hadn't planned to go anywhere with this woman. There was no place he could find peace right now, but he especially didn't want her near the home he'd shared with Grace.

So why had he come here?

He glanced over at her, wondering how she fit into all this. It was no act of fate that she'd ended up in Whitehorse—or that she was the one someone had chosen to tell their secrets to. No coincidence at all.

And Andi Blake had to know it.

Chapter Seven

"Where are we?" Andi asked, squinting into the storm.

Cade had taken the back way into the cabin, circling around the north end of Nelson Reservoir, figuring he'd give her a taste of rural Montana in the winter. He took perverse satisfaction in the way she'd been forced to hang on.

As the cabin came into view and the frozen reservoir beyond it, he thought about the first time he'd laid eyes on Grace Browning.

He'd been driving northwest on Hwy 2 headed toward Saco when he'd seen her crouched beside her car just off the highway with a flat tire on the left rear.

He'd stopped, seeing that she appeared to be a woman alone, and got out to walk back to her.

She hadn't looked up, just flicked a glance at his boots before she said, "Thanks, but I've got it."

He'd smiled to himself. She was a little thing but she was tackling that flat tire as if she was a truck driver. He'd thought about telling her not to be ridiculous, to move aside and let him change it.

But he'd stood back instead and watched her, seeing how not only capable she was, but also how determined. If he'd learned anything about women it was to give them their space when they had that particular look in their eyes.

But he wasn't about to leave her alone on this empty stretch of highway. So he stood back and watched with a mixture of amusement and awe.

Now, though, he wondered if she hadn't wanted him to help her because she had something to hide. Like a trunkful of stolen cash and a bounty on her head.

Clearly she'd been hiding everything, he thought bitterly.

But a part of him argued that if she had the robbery money, why had she married him? Why had she stayed in Whitehorse, Montana? Why had she gotten pregnant with his child?

The memory was like a stake to his heart. His foot came off the gas, the pickup's front tires sliding off into the deep snow. He fought to wrestle the truck back into the tracks.

"Are you all right?" Andi asked beside him.

"Fine," he snapped. He'd thought he'd been grieving the last six years. It was nothing compared to now. At least he'd had his memories of Grace. And now even those were tainted because didn't common sense tell him that Grace had just been hiding out here, the marriage to him having just been a cover until she divvied up the money with her accomplice and split, just as Andi suspected?

But if Starr had had the money from the bank robberies in her trunk that day, what had she done with it? She'd have had to hide it somewhere, otherwise he would have known about it. Three million dollars wouldn't have fit in her purse. Or one of her shoe boxes.

And why the hell hadn't she just kept going?

She'd finished changing the tire, then looked up for the first time at him.

He'd been startled by the same thing that had given away her identification when Tex had seen her photograph in the newspaper clipping. Her eyes.

They were pale blue and bottomless.

"You're still here," she'd said, sounding amused. "Haven't you ever seen a woman change a tire before?"

"Not with that kind of determination," he admitted.

She'd laughed.

He'd often wondered if he'd fallen in love with her the moment he'd looked into her eyes—or if it had been when she'd laughed. Either way, it had been like a jolt of electricity straight to his heart.

The day had been hot and he'd said the first thing he'd thought to say.

"Buy you a beer at the bar up the road."

She'd smiled at him, those eyes twinkling. "A beer?" She'd nodded thoughtfully. "I could use a beer."

"Cade Jackson," he'd said and held out his hand.

"Grace Browning." Was that the moment her alias and her cover had been born? There had been no hesitation when she'd said the name, no clue that this woman was anything but who she said she was.

Or had he been so enamored that he just hadn't noticed?

A part of him hadn't expected her to follow him to the bar, let alone come in and have a beer with him.

But she had.

"You're from here," she'd said.

It really hadn't been a question, but he'd answered anyway. "Born and raised south of here on a ranch."

She'd eyed him for a moment. "So you really are a cowboy."

He'd laughed. "If you mean do I ride a horse, yes. My father sold the ranch, but I bought a smaller one to the north. I raise horses more as a sideline. The rest of the time I run a bait shop here in town."

He remembered her smile, the amusement that played in her eyes.

"Horses and a bait shop." She shook her head. "Diversification, huh. Well, Cade Jackson, that's quite a combination. You make any money at it?"

He remembered being a little defensive. "I have all I need."

Her expression had changed, her features softening. "I envy you. Most people never have enough."

"Most people want too much," he'd said.

He smiled at that now as he realized that the woman he'd said that to had more than three million dollars.

So why hadn't she kept on going down that highway? Why had she hung around to have another beer and dinner? Hung around long enough that he fell more deeply in love with her? Hung around long enough to get pregnant with his child?

"Starr could have kept on going," he said as he parked in front of the cabin. "Why didn't she?"

"You tell me," Andi said as he saw her look down the plowed road that led to the cabin, her eyes narrowing. "Do you think you can scare me into not doing the story?" she demanded, clearly irate.

Is that what he thought? Or was he just angry at the messenger? He reminded himself that she hadn't just brought him the bad news. She planned to *publicize* it. Once her story broke, the media would have a field day and he'd be right in the heart of the storm.

He knew then why he'd brought her here. He wanted her to know the woman he had. He wanted to convince Andi that Grace Browning had existed. And while a part of him knew he was wasting his time, he knew he had to try. Not so much for Andi as for himself.

"Grace could have chosen a life on the run with the money. She didn't. How do you explain that, Tex?" he asked as he cut the engine and turned his attention on her.

"I can't. So are you telling me that there weren't things she said or did that made you wonder if there wasn't more to her staying here? Things that made you worry she wasn't telling the truth?"

"Stop looking at me like I'm an idiot. I knew my wife. I'm not a fool."

And he'd known something was wrong. He'd seen her fighting a battle with herself. He just hadn't known what it was. Or how to help her. He'd hoped whatever had been haunting her would blow over. When she'd called from Billings about the baby, she'd sounded completely happy.

And he'd known then that she'd won whatever battle had been going on inside her. A battle he'd just assumed had something to do with another man.

Maybe he was a fool after all.

"Isn't it possible that Grace wanted to put her past behind her and start over?" he asked, hating the emotion he heard in his voice. "Isn't it possible that she was tired of that life, that she wanted something more, that she'd found it with me? That maybe Grace was exactly who I believed her to be?"

He knew what he was saying. That he and his love had changed Starr Calhoun into Grace Browning Jackson, a woman he would have died for.

Something caught his eye in the rearview mirror. The wind whipped the snow past and for just a moment he saw the glare off the windshield of a car on the road by the reservoir.

Earlier he'd had the strangest feeling that they were being followed. Crazy. This was Whitehorse. All this talk of outlaws was making him paranoid.

He lost sight of the vehicle in the falling snow and felt a wave of relief. But as he looked at Andi, he saw both skepticism—and pity—and felt his temper boil. Not only had she turned his life upside down, but she was also making him doubt everything—including the safety of the community he'd lived in his entire life.

"Maybe you just saw the woman she wanted you to see," Andi said.

"Were you this cynical before or does it come with

being a reporter?" he demanded with no small amount of disdain.

"Now who's being contemptuous? I'm proud of my profession."

He lifted a brow.

"People have the right to know the truth." She snapped. "If there weren't individuals willing to go out on a limb to get the truth, what would that leave?"

"Peace?" he asked with a laugh.

She scoffed. "Some people just can't take the truth obviously."

Obviously. "Truth is relative. Your truth apparently isn't mine because you're wrong about my wife." He could feel her gaze on him like a weight. "Maybe she was Starr Calhoun."

"Maybe?"

"You want to know about Grace Browning? Take this down, girl reporter. Grace was as different from Starr Calhoun as night and day." With that he opened his pickup door and climbed out.

ANDI HEARD how desperately he wanted to believe that Starr had changed before she died. That she'd become Grace Browning, the woman he'd fallen in love with. That Starr had wanted to put that other life behind her.

Who knows what Starr had been thinking when she hit Whitehorse? But Andi could see that Cade needed to believe that the woman had stayed because she'd fallen in love with him instead of merely using him and this place as a hideout like the outlaw she was.

As she watched Cade stride away from the pickup through the snow, she wondered. Had he grieved six years because he'd loved his wife that much? Or had his pain been one of disillusionment and denial?

"You knew her best," Andi said diplomatically as she caught up with him.

"I *did* know her," he said, stopping to turn to face her.

That was why she needed his part of the story. Not that she believed for a minute that Starr Calhoun had changed. How could someone go from being the cold-hearted, calculating criminal on the audio tape to becoming an upstanding citizen and a wife to this man in a matter of months?

But if true, it would make a great story.

Not that anyone would believe the transformation except Cade. Look at the woman's genes. Had anyone in the family stayed out of prison? Maybe Worth. Unfortunately that was hard to verify since he could be breaking the law at this moment just under another name.

Starr and a change of heart? No way. Not even for this good-looking cowboy, Andi thought.

As she followed him toward the small cabin, she wondered how Starr could have stayed as long as she did here. A woman used to big cities and everything stolen money could buy would have gone crazy here, wouldn't she have?

All Andi could figure is that Starr had been waiting for something. The money? Or for her brother Houston to meet up with her? Then where did Lubbock come in?

She doubted Starr would trust Houston to bring the

money. Rightly so apparently since Houston hadn't shown up. Or had he?

Andi's suspicious nature couldn't help but come back to Starr's death. Just as she worried about the person who had wanted her to know that Grace Jackson was really Starr Calhoun.

She was still going with the theory that Starr had staged her death and taken off with the money and that someone possibly in Starr's own family might be looking for her and using Andi to do it.

Cade had stopped at the edge of the porch and was looking back at her. He didn't seem like anybody's fool, she thought. So how had Starr tricked him into not only buying her act, but also falling madly in love with her and now defending her even when he knew who she really had been?

Andi saw him frown as he looked past her back up the road from the way they'd come.

"Is something wrong?" she asked, turning to follow his gaze. Through the falling snow she caught the glint of the dull gray light off a vehicle just before it disappeared over a hill.

"I think we might have been followed," he said distractedly but she could tell he was worried. She recalled how he'd been watching his rearview mirror earlier. Or maybe he was just trying to scare her.

"I didn't see anyone." She was still irritated that he'd taken some back road through the deep snow no doubt just to frighten her. But she felt a stab of apprehension as she realized they could have been followed.

The cabin couldn't have been in a more deserted place. She shivered as she stared through the falling snow at the reservoir and saw an ice-fishing shack not far off shore. She realized it must be Cade's since there was no sign of anyone else around.

What an isolated place, she thought as she clutched her shoulder bag to her side, slipping her hand in to make sure she had her new can of pepper spray.

CADE WAITED TO SEE if the vehicle he'd spotted earlier drove by again. Could just be someone lost since no one used this road this time of year. From this side of the reservoir, there was no way to drive out onto the ice.

Other than ice fishing, there wasn't any other reason to come down this road since it ended at the bottom of a rocky outcropping.

If not someone lost, then they had been followed. Which would mean Andi Blake might actually know what she was talking about. In which case, there just might be cause for concern.

"You realize you're being used," he said. She didn't answer. "Aren't you worried as hell what this person wants and what he'll do when he doesn't get it?"

"What do you suggest I do?"

He ignored the sarcasm in her tone. "Go back to Texas. Forget you ever saw that clipping or heard that tape."

She raised a brow. "And what will you do? Can you just forget it? I didn't think so."

"I'll turn it over to my brother because frankly, I don't give a damn what happened to the money." His gaze fell on her. "But you're in it for the story to the bitter end, aren't you? Whoever is feeding you the information knows that. They know you won't back down."

"And they're right."

He shook his head.

"Do you really think they are just going to let me stop now?" she asked.

"You're in *danger.*"

"Not as long as I keep digging until I find what that person wants."

"You think you're going to find the money." He let out a laugh. "That's the topping on your story, isn't it?"

What had he been thinking bringing her to the cabin he and Grace had shared. It felt like a betrayal. The thought made him want to laugh. Grace had *betrayed* him.

He scowled over at Andi. What did any of us know about each other really? All his instincts told him that Andi Blake had her own secrets—but not for long. At this very moment, his brother was working on finding out everything there was to know about her.

And Cade was anxious to know. He knew he was looking for some kind of leverage. So far Andi Blake had been holding all the cards.

"What are we doing here?" she asked impatiently.

What were they doing here? He'd thought maybe here, in the home that he and Grace had shared, would be proof that Grace Browning had existed. But the only proof was what he felt in his heart and even he was starting to question whether it had been real.

As Andi had pointed out, the three million dollars was still missing. Apparently someone was looking for it. And Andi Blake wasn't the only one who knew about Grace being Starr.

Something had happened in Texas to catapult her to Montana. He'd bet the ranch on it. He had a bad feeling whatever it was would end up being connected to Starr and the Calhoun family.

He thought about turning around and going back to town. But he'd come this far…

"Come on," he said. "You want to know about Grace…" He headed toward the arena, not ready to take Andi inside the cabin, if ever.

"Where are the horses?" she asked once inside. He'd taken his time showing her around, stalling.

"I board them during the winter," he said. The truth was he had boarded them in town ever since Grace died, avoiding the cabin and thoughts of the future they had planned here.

It was cold in the arena. He could see his breath and Andi wasn't dressed for winter in Montana. The fool woman was still wearing that lightweight leather coat and high-heeled boots. She was shivering, her teeth practically chattering. She had her arms wrapped tightly around herself and looked as if she was close to hypothermia.

He swore silently. Whatever animosity he felt toward her for coming into his life and blowing it all to hell, he hadn't meant to let her freeze.

"You look cold," he said.

"I'm fine."

Her teeth were chattering now.

"Right," he said. "Come on." There would be no getting out of it. He'd have to take her into the cabin and get her warmed up before they headed back to town.

For just an instant it crossed his mind how alike Grace and Andi had been when it came to stubborn determination.

He quickly pushed that thought away with distaste. Andi was nothing like Grace. At least the Grace he'd thought he'd married.

"WHAT IS that?" Andi asked, trying to keep her mind off the freezing cold as they walked toward the cabin. The snow was deep and the ice under it slick. She couldn't feel her fingers in her leather gloves. Nor her toes in her boots.

"What?" He stopped to look back at her.

She pointed in the distance to what appeared to be the skeleton of a house someone had started and abandoned. The wood was weathered gray against a backdrop of rocky bluffs.

"I was building a bigger place for us when Grace was killed," he said, following her gaze.

"You plan to finish it?"

"No."

"So you're just going to leave it like that? I would think it would only act as a constant reminder of what you'd lost."

He turned to glare at her. "I don't know what I'm going to do with it, all right? What's it to you anyway?"

"Nothing. I was just curious," she said.

"Maybe one of these days I'll raze it. Happy?" With that he turned and strode off toward the cabin.

She stared at his strong back, the determined set of his shoulders and shook her head. Would she ever understand this man?

Reminding herself that she didn't need to understand him, she tucked the information away, already weaving it along with this place into her story as she trailed after Cade, colder than she'd ever been in her life.

A gust of wind whirled snow into her face as she neared the house. She felt her boot heel slip on the ice and would have gone down if Cade hadn't grabbed her.

He shook his head in apparent amused disgust as he took her leather gloved hand and led her up the steps to the cabin.

She drew her hand back once they were on the porch, angry with herself and with him. She was out of her realm—just as he would be in Fort Worth. So she hadn't walked on anything but sidewalk most of her life. So she was cold and not as surefooted on the ice as he was. She didn't need his condescending attitude.

As he unlocked the front door of the cabin, she realized she could no longer feel her feet. And she couldn't stop shaking.

Cade ushered her inside where the interior of the cabin was only a little warmer than the arena.

Andi stood just inside the door looking around. She hadn't been sure what to expect. The outside of the cabin was rustic, appearing to have been built back in the 1930s. It was log-framed with chinking between the logs and a weathered rail porch, all grayed with age.

So it was a surprise to see that the inside of the cabin was quite homey. She instantly recognized a woman's touch—this cabin was so different from the apartment where Cade stayed in town behind the bait shop.

Cade must have noticed her startled expression. "It was all Grace's doing."

The decor was warm and inviting with comfortable furniture and welcoming colors. Also the place was more spacious than she would have guessed from the outside.

There was a rock fireplace against one wall with book-shelves on both sides to the ceiling. She walked over to glance at the books. They all looked as if they'd been read, and more than once. The variety of topics surprised her given that a cowboy and a bank robber had lived here. She looked up to find Cade's dark gaze on her.

"Most of the books are mine." He sounded defensive. "Or didn't you think I could read?"

She ignored that as she moved around, trying to warm up her hands and feet. What had she been thinking moving to Montana in the middle of winter? It was literally freezing up here.

She pulled several books from the shelves, then put them back.

"I'll make us some coffee," he said, then seemed to hesitate. "Maybe I'd better make a fire."

She glanced around as he got a blaze going in the fireplace. All of the walls had interesting black and white photographs of what she assumed was the area.

They had such a Western feel to them that Andi was reminded of old movies she'd watched as a child with her father. He loved Roy Rogers and Gene Autry films.

"Grace took those," Cade said behind her.

It surprised her that Starr was such a good photographer. "I had no idea Starr was this talented."

Cade met her gaze. "There's a lot you didn't know about my wife."

Apparently so. But a lot he didn't know, either.

"She was going to have a show in Great Falls in the spring. She was shy about her work, but I talked her into it." He stopped as if he realized another reason Starr might not have wanted to go public with her work.

"Wrap up in that quilt on the couch. You need to warm your fingers and toes slowly otherwise they'll hurt," he said as he turned and went into the kitchen.

Her fingers and toes already ached from the cold. She couldn't imagine them hurting any worse as she went to stand by the blaze he'd gotten going in the fireplace.

Within moments, she felt a painful tingling in her fingers. Her toes were starting to tingle, as well. She could hear him banging around in the kitchen. She sat down on the couch, her eyes tearing with the pain.

Why had he brought her here? She pulled her shoulder bag with the pepper spray in it closer—just in case she might need it, then wrapped the quilt around her, wondering if Starr had made it as she stared into the flames.

Cade came out of the kitchen and handed her a mug of steaming instant coffee.

Her hands and feet hurt, just as he said they would. She grimaced as she wrapped her fingers around the hot mug.

"Here," he said. "We need to get those wet boots off." Before she could protest he knelt in front of her and taking one of her boots in both hands began to unzip them. "If you're going to live here, you've got to dress for the weather."

"I'm fine," she lied and attempted to pull her foot back.

He gave her an impatient look, pulled off her boot, then reached for the other one. He removed the second boot, put both boots to warm near the fire and began to gently rub her feet.

"They're hurtin', aren't they?" he said, nodding before she could answer. "They'll be better in a minute."

She'd have to take his word for it. She sipped her coffee, trying to ignore the feel of his strong but gentle fingers rubbing her feet.

The cabin felt much smaller. Cade Jackson seemed to fill the entire space with his very male presence. She knew how much this was hurting him, being here in his cabin he'd shared with his wife. Clearly he didn't spend much time here since her death. Andi could tell that he'd been reluctant to bring her here. So why had he? As hard as he tried not to show it, she could see that this was killing him.

"Better?" he asked after a few minutes.

She nodded. "Thank you." The moment he stood again, she tucked her feet under her. Not that she didn't appreciate his kindness. As she sipped her coffee she watched him. He stood next to the fireplace, the flames playing on his strong features.

Had Starr fallen so deeply in love with this man that she really had wanted to change? As Andi studied him, she thought it actually possible. There was something so comforting about this man, a strength, and yet an aliveness that drew even her.

"What now?" Cade asked quietly.

She shook her head, not understanding since only moments before her thoughts had been on anything but Starr and the news article she would write.

"I've shown you my life with Grace," he said. "You can do your story. What else do you want from me?"

There was one thing she needed before she broke the story, but she knew it would be over Cade Jackson's dead body.

However, none of this felt as if it was in her hands anymore—if it ever had been. She was being led by whoever was providing her with the information. That person knew her, knew that this was personal for her, knew she wouldn't quit until she got to the truth.

"It isn't about what I want," she said, believing that to be true. "Whoever is supplying me with the information, wants something."

He nodded solemnly. "The money." He said it with such distaste she didn't doubt he'd never seen it let alone spent it.

"That would be my guess," she said.

"We already know that." Cade rubbed a hand over his face in frustration. "But I don't know where the money is. If Starr had it, I was never aware of it."

She nodded. "I believe that. The question is, does Starr still have it?"

"You're not back to your theory that Starr walked away from that wreck, are you?"

Her gaze locked with his. "What if she isn't dead? What if you didn't bury your wife? Then she is alive somewhere with your child. We need to know if that body you buried is actually Starr's. You're the only one who can have her body exhumed."

Cade froze, his mug partway to his mouth, his eyes suddenly hard as stones.

Andi rushed on, "If her DNA matches that of one of her brothers in prison—"

He threw the mug with enough force that it shattered when it hit the wall. Coffee made a dark stain across the woodwork and floor.

Without a word, he stormed out of the cabin.

Chapter Eight

"You can go visit my cousin in Minnesota until the baby is born and then come back," Arlene said.

Charlotte looked up at her from the couch where she was eating cold leftover pancakes dripping with syrup. "I'm not going anywhere. It's not like everyone doesn't already know I'm pregnant."

"What about the father?" Arlene asked, wiping up crumbs from the plastic on the couch beside her daughter.

"What about him?" Charlotte asked, licking her fingers.

"Have you told him the baby's his?"

Charlotte turned her attention to the last pancake on the plate. She dredged it through a lake of syrup but didn't lift it to her mouth. "He doesn't believe me that it's his."

"And you're *protecting* this man?" Arlene demanded. "What is wrong with you?"

"Nothing. It's my baby. I *want* it."

Arlene raised a brow. "Want it? What do you intend to *do* with it?"

"Raise it," Charlotte snapped.

"You? Raise a baby?"

"I figure I can do a hell of a lot better than you have," her daughter said, shoving away her plate. The pancake spilled to the floor in a pool of syrup as Charlotte stormed off to her bedroom, slamming the door solidly behind her.

Arlene stared down at the pancake and syrup soaking into the rug for a moment, then dropped to her knees to hurriedly clean up the mess. She'd always kept a clean house, prided herself in her neatness. Floyd had hated the way she fussed around the house.

"Sit down, for cripe's sake, Arlene," he'd bark. "You're driving me crazy with your cleaning."

Nervous energy. She'd always had more than her share.

She scrubbed at the rug, frantic to get the syrup up before it stained the rug, wondering why she'd tried so hard. She'd wanted to be a good wife and mother. Her own mother had been cold and uncaring. Arlene had never been able to do anything right according to her.

She quit scrubbing at the rug. The dishrag felt sticky in her hands. Her eyes burned hot. She couldn't remember the last time she'd cried and was surprised when scalding tears began to run down her face.

Her body shook with chest-rattling sobs. Through blinding tears, she saw herself on the floor crying as a child, her mother standing over her.

Her mother had always said Arlene wouldn't amount to anything. Even when Arlene had kept her house and her kids spotless, her mother had found fault until the day she died.

But that day, on the floor, her mother standing over her with the leather strap, Arlene had prayed that she could prove her mother wrong as she cried for the father she'd never known to save her.

He hadn't and her mother's prophecy had now come true. Arlene Evans was a disgrace, a failed wife, a failed mother. How could she allow another generation to be born into this mess?

ANDI STARED after Cade as a gust of cold air blew in with the slamming of the door.

She'd known he wasn't going to take the idea of the exhumation well. Not that she blamed him. She found she was shaking and wondered if it was from his reaction—or her own. She'd just asked a man to dig up his dead wife, a woman he had clearly loved almost more than life itself.

She felt sick. Had she no compassion anymore? Not for the Calhouns. And even less for Starr who had obviously broken Cade Jackson's heart—and Andi feared would completely destroy it by the time this was finished.

She hated being a part of it. But she was and had been for more years than she wanted to admit.

Not that she thought the person who sent her the clippings and tape would let her stop now anyway. How far was he willing to go to get what he wanted? And what exactly did he want besides the money?

She rose from her chair in front of the fire to retrieve her boots. They felt warm as she slipped her feet into them. As she did, she noticed a row of books—all about the outlaws of the Old West.

Andi pulled down one with a well-used paperback cover and thumbed through it, stopping on the title page. It was signed: "Grace, I know how much you like these stories. Love, Cade."

She heard a sound outside the cabin and put the book back. Now she understood Cade's expression when he'd found her in the outlaw section at the museum. He'd known about Grace's interest in the outlaws of the Old West.

So what did that have to do with anything?

And where was Cade? she wondered as she took her mug to the kitchen. She rinsed it out and set it on the counter, admiring what Starr had done with the house.

Why had Starr bothered fixing up this place if she was planning to take off? Or had the decorating just been something to do until she could take the money and leave?

Andi cleaned up the broken mug and spilled coffee. Past the kitchen was an open door. Through it she could see the bedroom. The colors alone drew her toward the room. An antique high bed with an iron frame sat in the middle of the room. The iron bed had been painted white, stark next to the color-crazy quilt on the bed.

But it was the photograph over the bed that drew her. She moved closer. The shot was of Cade. Starr had captured the man so perfectly, both his strength and his stubbornness as well as a vulnerability that pulled at Andi's heart. This was the man Starr had fallen in love with. The man who had changed her into Grace Browning.

"Are you ready?"

Andi jumped at the sound of Cade's voice directly behind her. She'd been so taken with the photograph and what it said about Cade—and Starr—that she hadn't heard him come back. "It's a wonderful photo of you."

He said nothing as he waited for her to leave the room before he firmly closed the door behind them.

"I should get you back to town," he said, taking her coat from where he'd hung it earlier to dry.

She wanted to tell him she was sorry. Sorry for suggesting the exhumation. Sorry that she was the one who'd brought this to him. But what she was really sorry for was that she hadn't believed him that Starr had become the woman, Grace Browning, who he'd loved.

She understood his pain more acutely. It was another reason she said nothing as he drove her back to Whitehorse in a fierce silence that brooked no arguments or discussions.

CADE MENTALLY KICKED himself all the way back to town. What in the hell had he been thinking? All Tex cared about was her damned news story. Seeing the home Grace had made for him had only given the reporter something more to write about.

But now she wanted him to exhume Grace's body?

It had been all he could do not to dump her in a snowbank on the way back to town.

Fortunately she'd had the good sense not to say a word all the way back, otherwise he couldn't be responsible for what he would have done.

He dropped her off without a word at the newspaper office and drove toward the bait shop, still kicking himself.

As he drove home, Christmas music played from somewhere down the street. Everywhere he looked there were twinkling Christmas lights.

Grace had been so excited about their first Christmas together. She'd decorated the cabin and made sugar cookies and eggnog.

It had started snowing the week before Christmas that year. Grace had been like a little kid, catching snowflakes in her mouth, making snow angels out in the yard. She'd said she'd never seen that much snow before. He promised they would make a snowman when she got back from her shopping trip to Billings.

He had wanted to go with her, but she'd been insistent that she had to go alone.

"It's a surprise and you're not going to ruin it," she'd said. "The roads are plowed and sanded. I'll be careful." She'd kissed him, holding his face between her warm palms, those blue eyes of hers filling with tears.

"You make me happier than I ever dreamed possible," she'd said.

He shoved the memory away, no longer sure what had been a lie, and looked in his rearview mirror.

His mood didn't improve at the sight of his brother's patrol car behind him. With a curse, Cade pulled into the bait shop, his brother pulling in behind him.

"Where you been?" the sheriff asked after motioning for Cade to get into the patrol car.

Cade cringed under his brother's intent gaze as he

slid into the passenger seat. "Out to the cabin. Fishing." Why was he lying? Why didn't he just tell Carter he'd been with the reporter? "Why? What's going on?"

Carter had his bad news look on.

"Just tell me." Cade hadn't meant to sound so abrupt. "Is it about Grace. Or Andi?"

"Andi?"

"Miranda Blake," Cade snapped, knowing he'd given himself away. He already knew about Grace. What he didn't want, he realized with surprise, was bad news about Tex.

Cade wanted the news, short and sweet. He didn't want sympathy. Nor did he want to have to explain himself.

"I can't find any record of Grace Eden Browning," his brother said. Carter looked more than a little uncomfortable. "No record of any kind. All I can figure is that she must have been born under another name. Do you happen to have her social security number?"

Cade shook his head. This wasn't news but hearing it from the sheriff definitely made it all the more real. "I'll see if I can find it. I'm sure there's an explanation."

"Yeah." Carter didn't sound convinced. "You don't seem surprised by this."

Cade knew it was just a matter of time before he was going to have to tell his brother the truth. But not yet. "What did you come up with on Miranda Blake?"

Carter seemed a little taken aback that Cade appeared more interested in Ms. Blake than this news about his former wife, but opened his notebook and said, "As for Miranda Blake…"

Cade listened, not surprised that Andi had been a top news anchorwoman in Fort Worth, working her way up as an investigative reporter and making quite a name for herself.

But her reason for leaving Fort Worth did surprise him.

"She took the job up here to get away from a stalker. Apparently one of her viewers had a crush on her," Carter said. "At first he sent her flowers, candy, love letters all anonymously. But when she asked him on the air to please stop, he felt rejected and started threatening her."

"Didn't she contact the police?" Cade asked.

The sheriff nodded. "But it's hard to catch these kinds of secret admirers. The threats escalated and she left the station. Not even her former boss knew where she'd gone."

"You didn't tell him where she was," Cade said, unable to hide his fear for Andi.

His brother looked even more surprised. "He knew I was with the Phillips County Sheriff's Department in Montana, but I doubt he was her secret admirer."

Still, Cade couldn't help being concerned.

"Her boss said they are holding her job for her for six months," his brother was saying. "That's why I would hate to see you get involved with this woman since you know she won't be staying for probably even that long."

Cade wanted to laugh out loud, but he had to go on letting his brother think his interest in Andi was romantic for a while longer.

"Don't worry," he told Carter. "I've already figured that out. I just thought it would be smart to know what I was dealing with."

His brother eyed him. "Dealing with?"

Cade shrugged and looked away, realizing he'd been too truthful. "Well, it has been a while since I've... dated."

"Yeah," Carter agreed quickly. "You'll want to take it slow." But he sounded pleased that Cade might even be thinking of dating again.

He felt a little guilty for leading his brother on like that. But in time, he would have to confide in Carter on a professional basis.

Cade didn't want to spoil the holidays. This could wait until after then. Until after his brother popped the question to Eve Bailey. Cade just hoped to hell she accepted Carter's proposal. There was enough heartbreak as it was.

"I'm glad you're doing better. I really am," his brother said. "I've been worried about you."

Cade knew he'd put his family through a lot. "I'm sorry I haven't been around much for you."

"Hey, I'm not complaining," Carter said. "I know you've been through hell." He smiled. "Just don't forget Christmas Eve. Unless I lose my nerve."

"You won't," Cade assured him. "You and Eve are made for each other."

"You care about this Andi Blake," Carter said.

He nodded. He could have argued the point, but didn't.

"Just be careful, okay?" his brother said. "I don't want to see you get hurt."

Carter had no idea just how he'd been hurt by the woman. "Don't worry. I know what I'm doing."

Carter didn't look as if he believed him.

"I have another favor," Cade said, quickly changing the subject. "I was hoping you could find out about a woman named Starr Calhoun for me."

His brother's expression didn't change. "Starr Calhoun?"

"She was originally from Texas."

"Texas? Like Miranda Blake," Carter said.

"Yeah. Thanks for doing this." Cade reached for the door and opened it.

Carter reached past him and closed it. "When are you going to be honest with me and tell me what's really going on?"

Cade felt the full weight of his brother's gaze. He squirmed. "Soon. Just trust me a little longer?"

Carter met his gaze and held it. "I'll trust you. But I have to know. Are you involved in anything illegal?"

"No." Not unless you considered withholding evidence illegal.

A WINTER STORM warning alert had been put out for Whitehorse and all counties east of the Rockies. With the blowing and drifting snow, the road south of Whitehorse was closed to all but emergency traffic.

Andi did what she had to at the newspaper, then headed back to her apartment. In this part of the county during winter, it got dark shortly after 4:30 p.m.

Once home, she got out of her cold car since the drive hadn't been far enough for the engine to even warm up a little. Snow fell silently around her. She didn't want to go up to her apartment, but she had nowhere else to go.

And while she was too upset to sit still, she didn't feel like unpacking any boxes. She wasn't even sure why she'd brought so much stuff. She wouldn't be staying. Especially the way she was feeling right now.

She was cold and tired and sick at heart as she climbed the stairs to her second-story apartment. Her thoughts kept coming back to Cade Jackson. He was a victim in all this. And the woman who'd involved him was allegedly dead and buried. Andi could understand how Cade didn't want to exhume the body of the woman he'd loved.

But how could he still love a woman who had deceived him the way Starr had? And wouldn't he need to know if she'd pulled a disappearing act, possibly with his baby?

The moment she flipped the light switch and nothing happened Andi knew someone was there in the dark waiting for her just as the man had been in Texas.

He came out of the blackness. She felt the air around her move an instant before he was on her. She caught his scent, a mix of body odor and cheap aftershave.

He slammed her back into the wall, knocking the air out of her, his fingers closing around her throat.

She tried to call out, but she had no breath and the pressure on her throat choked off any sound. She scratched at his face, only to get a handful of thick mask.

He let go of her throat with one hand and slapped her hand away, wrestling her arms behind her as he pinned her body to the wall, his fingers digging into her throat.

She'd been wrong. It wasn't her attacker from Texas. This man was larger, stronger. She couldn't breathe.

"Listen, bitch. Hurry up and find the money like you're supposed to. Run and I'll track you down and kill you. Don't even think about telling your friend's cop brother."

At the sound of pounding footsteps on the stairs to her apartment, he loosened his hold, then slammed her hard against the wall before letting her go. "I'll be in touch."

She saw stars. She gasped for breath, her throat on fire. Her legs gave out. As she slid down the wall to the floor someone burst into the apartment. She caught the glint of a star—and a weapon.

"Help." The word came out in a whisper. But even as she said it, she knew that her attacker was gone. She could feel the cold breeze blowing across the floor and knew the back door was open.

"Stay with her," the man with the badge ordered as he turned on a flashlight and swept the beam across her small apartment. She looked away, blinded by the sudden light.

"Are you all right?" The voice surprised her. Just as Cade did as he knelt down next to her.

She looked up into his face and began to shake. He gently pulled her toward him.

"It's okay," he said as he rubbed her back.

His kindness brought the tears. She hated this feeling of weakness, and worse letting him see her like this. She'd always had to be strong. For her mother. For herself because there was no one else.

"You're okay," he said, as if he knew how hard it was for her to be vulnerable in front of him.

She leaned into his strength, no longer able to fight back her emotions as she remembered the man's threat—and the sensation of knowing she was going to die if she didn't get air.

The lights flickered on. She pulled herself together and Cade handed her a tissue from the end table nearby.

"How is she?" the sheriff asked standing over them.

Cade got to his feet, gently pulling her up and easing her over to the couch. "Give her a minute."

"I'm all right." Her voice came out in a whisper. She was far from all right.

The sheriff took out his notebook. "I'm going to need to ask you some questions. I'm Sheriff Carter Jackson, Cade's brother."

She nodded and told him about reaching for the light. When it hadn't gone on, she'd known someone was in her apartment.

"How did you make the call?"

She shook her head. "I didn't." She'd wondered how they'd gotten to her so quickly. She saw the sheriff exchange a look with his brother.

"I was with my brother when he got the call about the break-in," Cade said as if seeing her confusion.

"Someone must have seen him break in." It hurt to talk. She swallowed, her eyes tearing from the pain.

The sheriff looked up from his notebook. "Is your apartment number 555-0044?" he asked.

She nodded numbly, knowing what was coming.

"According to the dispatcher, the call came from that number. From inside your apartment."

She felt her eyes widen in alarm. "I don't understand."

"Neither do I," the sheriff said as he walked into her

kitchen and picked up the phone near the back door and hit Redial.

She watched his face, knew the emergency operator had answered.

"This is Sheriff Jackson. I was just testing the line." He hung up and looked at Andi. "The last call made was to the 911 operator. If you didn't make the call from here, then who did?"

Chapter Nine

"What the hell was that about in there?" Cade demanded the moment he and his brother were outside again. "Did you see her throat? She was *attacked*. You're acting as if she staged the whole thing."

Carter said nothing as he opened the door of his patrol car. "You want a ride home?"

"No, I want you to tell me what the hell is going on."

"I don't know," his brother said calmly. "I just know that the 911 call originated inside that apartment. Either she made the call, or her attacker did."

"That's crazy. Did the dispatcher say whether it was a man or a woman on the phone?"

"The voice was muffled."

Cade swore. "You should be out looking for her attacker."

Carter was studying him. "This has something to do with why you wanted me to check on her, doesn't it?"

"Forget it," Cade said, holding up his hands in surrender as he backed away from the patrol car. "There's no talking to you."

"Try telling me what's going on with you and that woman in there. She's trouble. Can't you see that?"

Carter called after him as he headed down the street. "Come on, I'll give you a ride."

Cade didn't answer as he kept walking toward home and his truck. He didn't know what to think, but he wasn't leaving her alone tonight.

ANDI BOLTED the door behind the sheriff and Cade. She was still shaken but the sheriff had checked the apartment and assured her there was no one in it. He'd found a window that had been ajar and shut it for her.

The sheriff had offered to take her to the emergency room to have her throat checked, but she'd declined. It was feeling better and she didn't want to be seen with the sheriff after the threat her attacker had made.

Lubbock Calhoun. That's who it had to have been. Hadn't she suspected once she'd learned he was out of prison and on the loose that he was the one sending her the information?

She shuddered at the memory of his hands on her throat. Why did he think *she* could find the money? This was crazy, but no crazier than her coming to Montana because of the Calhouns. This is where her obsession had gotten her—in worse trouble than she could imagine. Bradley was right. She should never have come up here.

She had to get out of Montana. But even as she thought it, she reminded herself that she'd already run from trouble in Texas. She'd thought she was safe here in Whitehorse, Montana. But Lubbock had found her.

She remembered what he'd said and began to shake. *Hurry up and find the money like you're supposed to.* Like you're supposed to?

Was it possible someone had tricked her into coming here? Feeding on her obsession with the Calhoun family?

Her heart began to beat harder. The stalker in Texas. "Oh, no." She put her hand over her mouth, tears burning her eyes. She'd been set up from the beginning. First the stalker to scare her out of Texas, then the job ad that had been sent to her.

Whoever had done it had known that she'd been running scared and had wanted to get away from Texas. She would never have come to Montana if Lubbock hadn't been arrested just miles from here.

She shook her head. She'd been set up. By Lubbock? It was too preposterous that a man like Lubbock Calhoun had planned this, manipulating her through each step to the point where he would physically threaten her into finding the money? As if she could.

She tried to imagine the man who'd almost strangled her to death having the patience to lay the groundwork to get her here and couldn't. It would have had to have been someone in Texas. Someone who knew her. Someone…

Fear curdled her stomach as she dug out her cell phone.

Bradley answered on the first ring. "I'm so glad you called. I have news."

She said nothing, all her fears growing inside her. Bradley knew her better than anyone. He was the one person who knew about her obsession with the Calhouns and how she would jump at a chance at retribution. But he'd also fanned the fires of her terror when her secret admirer had become a stalker. He'd encouraged her to leave Texas, for her own safety. If Bradley had hired someone to stalk her…

"Are you all right? You sound funny," he asked as if hearing the change in her.

"News?" she said, her voice breaking. How could she be thinking these things about her friend? Her closest friend?

"Great news," Bradley said with a flourish. "There's been an arrest. The police found your stalker."

"What?" It was the last thing she'd expected. She dropped into a chair.

"And wait until you hear who it is." He did a drumroll. So like Bradley to play the moment to the hilt. "Rachel, your nemesis. That's right, sweetie. The police found evidence in her locker—and in her boyfriend's car. She got her boyfriend to do the dirty deed."

"Rachel?" Andi was still in shock. "Why would she—"

"Isn't it obvious? She wanted your job—and it worked like a charm, didn't it? She continued sending the threats hoping you wouldn't return and the newscaster job would become permanent."

Andi didn't know what to say. Her whole theory that there had been an elaborate plot to get her to Montana came unraveled. Just moments before she'd been suspecting Bradley… She began to cry.

"Sweetie, I thought you'd be *happy* to hear this."

"I am," she managed to say. "I'm just so relieved." So

relieved that her stupid suspicions were unfounded and feeling guilty for even having them. "Rachel confessed?"

"*Right,* sweetie. She's denying everything and so is her boyfriend but the police found enough evidence between the two of them so it's a slam dunk and truthfully, no one at the station is surprised in the least. So now you can come back to Texas. Your old job is waiting for you—and you have one fantastic story to break."

She didn't know how to tell him. "There's news up here as well."

"You sound funny. Are you all right?"

She told him about the attack.

"That's it," he said. "You're getting out of there."

"If I thought there was someplace I could run and get away from him, I would."

"You're that convinced it was Lubbock Calhoun?"

"Yes." Her throat was sore and painful again. "I shouldn't talk anymore."

"Then just listen," Bradley said. "I have some more news although I was hoping you'd forget about the Calhouns and just come home. But the robbery money? It's never turned up. At least none of the 'bait' money. I'm betting one of them hid it and for one reason or another couldn't get back to it. Which could explain why Lubbock, if that's who it is, put you on Starr's trail."

What he said made sense. "Bradley, I feel as if I've been set up. I knew someone was pulling my strings once I got here, but I think it goes deeper than that." She told him what Lubbock—if that's who it had been—had said to her.

"I didn't want to say anything, but I think you're

dead-on," Bradley said. "It seemed pretty obvious why. They have to know who you are, your connection to their family, and given the amount of exposure you've gotten in Texas…"

"But why would they think I could find the money? That's just crazy."

"Are you serious? Look, I've given this some thought. What else do I have to do at work all day?" he joked. "Number one, Lubbock sure as the devil couldn't get close to Cade Jackson, but you can. Two, you're trained to get information. Look at the stories you broke, including that famous murder case that you practically solved single-handedly."

She groaned, realizing that there were viewers out there who thought they knew her.

"The good news is that it must mean that there is information to be found," he was saying. "Whoever is after the money, Lubbock or Houston or even Starr possibly if you're right and she faked her death, know who you are. They're using you, kiddo. Maybe even one of them got to Rachel for all we know."

She felt sick. "How am I going to find the money?"

"The same way you go after news stories," Bradley said. "If anyone can do this, it's you."

"You haven't seen this country. It's vast and right now it's covered in snow. A lot of it looks the same. It would be so easy to get lost in."

"Exactly," he said, sounding excited. "You've just hit the nail on the head. The Calhouns would have had the same problems when they hid that money."

Even as exhausted and scared as she was, she saw where he was going with this. "You think they would have made a map back to the money."

Bradley laughed. "Isn't that what you would have done? So now all you have to do is find the map. Don't thank me yet," he joked.

"It seems like a lot of trouble to go to," she said. "Why didn't Starr just split the money with Houston and skip the country?"

"Don't forget Lubbock. He would have wanted a taste and I have a feeling him being arrested on that old warrant near Whitehorse was no coincidence. I'm betting the cops got an anonymous tip."

"Starr?"

"That would take care of one brother for six years," Bradley said. "Now all she had to do was contend with Houston. So she hid the money where she's the only one who knows how to find it. Gives her leverage."

Especially if Cade was right and she wanted to start her life over. But then why not give up all the money?

"I'm not so sure about the map, sorry," she said. "Wouldn't Cade have found it by now if there'd been one?"

"It wouldn't have been something obvious," Bradley said. "It would have to be disguised as something else."

Andi laughed. It felt good to talk to him even if it did hurt her throat a little. "You're really getting into this, aren't you?"

"I can't help it. I'm down here where it's safe and

I can live vicariously through you," he said. "Aren't you scared?"

"Terrified. I'm afraid the Calhouns think I'm a lot smarter than I actually am."

"I'd argue that. But you can quit, go to the cops, get out of there. Just tell me what time I should pick you up at the airport."

"You know I'm no quitter and quite frankly I'm afraid to go to the cops. The ones in Fort Worth certainly didn't do much to find my stalker when I was down there." She didn't mention that the sheriff up here was more suspicious of her than her attacker because of a phone call she couldn't explain.

If she told Sheriff Jackson what she was really thinking about this whole mess, she knew he'd be as disbelieving as she was.

"You are so much braver than I would be," Bradley said.

"Goes without saying," she joked, so glad her fears about him were baseless. Talking to Bradley, it was easy to forget the trouble she was in. At least for a while. "I do miss you."

"Good. So keep in touch, okay? Call me every day. I need to know that you're all right. And be careful of this Cade Jackson character. I think he knows more than he's telling you. I'd hate to see you get taken in by a pretty face."

She thought of Cade, remembering his expression when he'd seen her looking at the outlaw exhibit. There was no doubt that he knew more than he was telling her.

"You're probably right," she said noncommittally as she thought of the way he'd rubbed her feet, the way he'd thrown the mug of coffee and stomped out at even the suggestion of digging up his wife's grave and how he'd held her earlier after the attack.

"I do love a treasure hunt. Except for the fact that it's a killer sending you the clues."

She groaned. "I thought gay men are supposed to be so sensitive?"

He laughed. "Sleep tight. And by all means, be careful."

After she hung up, she wished for a moment that she'd taken the sheriff's advice. "You might consider staying at a motel tonight if you don't feel safe here," he'd said before he left.

She'd seen his suspicion. He didn't believe that she hadn't made the call. She couldn't blame him. It made no sense to her, either. Why would Lubbock make the call? Unless someone else had been in her apartment.

With the blinds closed and the doors locked, she had to check the apartment again for herself. She didn't expect her attacker to return. He wanted the money. His threat had been strong enough that he didn't need to come back tonight to make sure she got the message.

She knew she should have told the sheriff everything. But then she would have to tell him the rest of it and she didn't doubt that Lubbock's threat was more of a promise. A man like Lubbock Calhoun could and would carry out that promise.

Look what had happened in Texas with her stalker.

The police hadn't been able to protect her. Nor had they caught the people behind it until after she left—and as Bradley said, it was so obvious who had the most to gain with her gone. If the police hadn't been able to catch Rachel until now, then Andi had even less faith that the local sheriff could stop someone like Lubbock Calhoun.

At least the stalker had been caught. She still felt guilty about her suspicions about Bradley. Thank goodness she hadn't voiced them.

She turned on the television, found an old Western, Bradley's favorite, and curled up to watch it, knowing she would never be able to sleep.

She was still shocked about Rachel even though she'd known how ambitious and competitive the woman had always been.

A little after midnight, though, Andi's apartment windows began to rattle from the wind. Snow pelted the glass that had already frosted over. She scraped at the frost on the inside of the glass, trying to see out. But she couldn't even see across the street because of the falling and drifting snow.

She realized she couldn't tell if Lubbock Calhoun or anyone else was out there watching her apartment. But as a gust of wind whirled snow down the street, she saw a familiar pickup parked directly below her window. Cade?

Andi told herself it couldn't be, but secretly she hoped it was him keeping a vigil over her.

She finally fell asleep in the wee hours of the morning, after she'd talked herself out of going down and seeing if Cade was in that pickup. What would she do if he was? Invite him up?

CADE SPENT the night in his pickup parked outside Andi's apartment. He was angry at his brother but after he'd cooled down, he had to admit he had a lot of questions himself.

If this was the stalker from Texas, then why hadn't Andi mentioned it to his brother? Instead she'd acted like she didn't know who had attacked her.

He'd seen how scared she'd been. Wasn't it time to tell Carter everything? And yet, he hadn't spoken up either, he reminded himself.

His sleeping bag was good to fifty below zero and he was damned glad of it. Snow swirled around the truck, burying it by morning.

Her light was on late into the night. He could see the flicker of her television screen. He took comfort in the fact that she couldn't sleep, either.

Several times he thought about going up to her apartment. He had a lot he wanted to talk to her about, including the attack and what she was keeping from him. His biggest fear was that the attack had something to do with Grace. And that damned money.

But he talked himself out of going upstairs. At this late hour and feeling the way he was toward her, going up to her apartment wasn't a good idea.

At one point, his brother had cruised by in his patrol car. Cade had slid down in his seat, but he was sure his brother had seen him—and thought him a fool.

THE NEXT MORNING Andi heard on the radio that because of the chill factor with the wind the temperature was twenty-four degrees below zero. She'd never been anywhere that cold and when she looked out the icy window she was startled to see that the snow had blown into huge sculpted drifts.

Cade's pickup was gone, she noted with a disappointment she had no business feeling. Her own car was buried in the snow, a huge drift completely hiding the rear of the car.

What was she doing here? All her life she'd felt more than able to handle anything that came her way. But she was completely out of her league. Not just that a hardened criminal was threatening her life. She wasn't prepared for this kind of weather.

This morning, her throat bruised and raw, she didn't feel strong enough to do this. She hated what she was doing to Cade Jackson. She was completely inept in this wild and dangerous country. And common sense told her she was so far in over her head that it was doubtful she'd get out of this alive.

Feeling the chill of the apartment, she turned up the heat and went to shower, angry with herself for bailing out of Texas. She'd jumped out of the frying pan and into the fire. If she hadn't run, none of this would be happening. But even as she thought it, she knew it wasn't true.

Come hell or high water, someone had been determined to get her here—and now she knew why. And she wasn't about to leave without the story.

When she came out of the shower after drying her

hair and dressing for work, she put on her warmest coat, hat, boots and gloves—which she knew would be sorely inadequate for this weather. Unfortunately she would have to wade through the drift to get to the hardware store to buy a snow shovel.

But when she opened the door she was shocked to see that a walkway had been carved through the drifted snow to her car.

The snow was piled deep on each side and as she neared the street and her car she saw snow flying through the air.

Closer she saw that someone with a shovel was on the other side of her car making that cloud of snow as they dug out her car. Some Good Samaritan. She only caught a glimpse of a stocking-capped head coming out of the cloud with each shovelful, but she was more than grateful for the help.

She'd reached the end of her car and had to yell to be heard over the howling wind and the scrape of the shovel.

The man stopped shoveling to turn around to look at her.

Cade Jackson. And he didn't look happy.

She couldn't have been more surprised. "What are you doing?"

"What does it look like?" he snapped and went back to shoveling.

"I could have done that myself," she hollered at him, wondering why he was angry with her. Because he'd had to sleep in his pickup last night in the cold? Whose idea had that been? Not hers.

"You have a snow shovel?" he asked as he stopped

to lean on his. "I didn't think so." He held out his hand. "Give me your keys. I doubt your car will start since you forgot to plug it in last night, but I'll try it for you."

Plug in her car? Was he joking?

He seemed to see her confusion.

"When it's this cold you have to get a head-bolt heater and plug your car in every night. Welcome to Montana."

She dropped her keys into his outstretched palm. "Thank you," she said meekly.

He grunted something she couldn't hear and handed her the snow shovel as he went to her car and tried to start the engine. The engine growled a few times.

"Come on," Cade said, getting back out of the car and slamming the door. "I'll give you a ride to work." Without waiting, he turned and started toward his pickup parked down the block, leaving her holding the snow shovel. "Keep the shovel, you're going to need it," he said over his shoulder.

Chilled to the bone, she wasn't about to argue as she stood the shovel against the wall of snow next to her apartment and hurried after Cade.

He'd left his pickup running. The inside of the truck was warm when she climbed in. She wanted to kiss him she was so glad to be inside somewhere warm. Just that few minutes outside had chilled her to the bone.

He glanced over at her as he put the truck in gear. "How ya like Montana now, Tex?"

"Just fine," she managed to say through her chattering teeth. "It's beautiful."

He smiled at that. "It's a lot prettier if you're properly

dressed. Stop by the department store. They'll get you outfitted. Unless of course you're having second thoughts about staying after what happened."

He'd stopped in front of the *Milk River Examiner* office. He glanced over at her. "Anything you want to tell me?"

"Thank you for the ride and the snow shovel," she said as she opened her door. She had to hang on to the handle to keep the door from blowing away. The cold took her breath away. "I'm not going anywhere."

"You might change your mind about that sooner than you think," he said and revved the engine.

She was already halfway out of the pickup or she would have demanded to know what that was about. As she hurried into the office and Cade Jackson sped away, she saw Sheriff Carter Jackson waiting for her inside.

CADE WENT BACK to the bait shop to find Harvey Alderson waiting in his pickup.

"'Bout time," Harvey said irritably and glanced at his watch.

"Kind of cold for ice fishing, isn't it, Harvey?" Cade said, opening the shop.

"It's warm in the icehouse," Harvey said and began going through the fish decoys before he began to inspect one of the spears.

It was clear to Cade that Harvey was just killing time and had no intention of buying anything let alone going spearfishing out on the reservoir even though the ice was plenty thick.

The moment Harvey left without buying anything,

Cade put up the Closed sign. He'd been mulling over everything his brother had told him, especially the part about Andi Blake.

Could he believe that a stalker had run her out of Texas and that she just happened to end up in White-horse, Montana?

He wondered if he was just a fool when it came to women. He'd believed Grace Browning was the woman she appeared to be. Look how wrong he'd been.

And now he'd bought into Andi Blake's story when clearly it was no coincidence the woman was here.

His head hurt from trying to sort it all out. Part of him wanted to go over to the newspaper office and get the truth out of her. But his good sense told him he needed to calm down, to figure a few things out before he talked to her again.

What he needed more than ever was to do the one thing that had kept him sane the last six years—fish. He'd always thought better out fishing.

"Ms. BLAKE," Sheriff Carter Jackson said, his hat in his hand. "I need to have a few words with you."

Andi glanced toward the back of the newspaper office. Empty. "Please have a seat," she said and turned back to lock the front door. "This won't take long, will it?"

He shook his head.

She felt his eyes on her as she walked over to her desk and sat down behind it. He pulled up a chair next to it.

"I would imagine you know why I'm here," the sheriff said.

She waited. It was a technique she'd learned quickly as a reporter. Let them do the talking.

"I know about the problems you had in Fort Worth," he said. "Why didn't you mention that you'd had a stalker after you in Texas yesterday when you were attacked?"

"I had no reason to connect the two," she said carefully.

He frowned. "Two different men are after you?"

"Actually I just learned last night that my stalker in Texas has been caught so there is no way it was the same man. It turned out to be the boyfriend of a coworker who apparently wanted my job."

"That's good news about the stalker being caught," the sheriff said. "May I see your throat?"

It was so badly bruised that she'd worn a turtleneck, not wanting to have to tell anyone about the attack. She pulled down the top of her turtleneck.

He whistled and shook his head. "That's some bruising you got there. It must hurt to talk. I'll try to make this quick. Did he say anything, make any kind of threat, demand your money?"

"You got there so quickly and scared him off, he really didn't have time to tell me what he had planned for me."

"Yeah," Carter said and scratched his jaw. "That phone call still bothers me."

"Me, as well." She made a point of looking at her watch.

"Am I keeping you from something?" he asked.

"I have an interview. If there isn't anything else…"

He studied her for a moment. His eyes weren't as

dark as his brother's and while he was probably the better looking of the two men, he didn't have the raw maleness that Cade had.

He slowly rose from the chair across from her desk. "What are your plans now?"

"My plans?"

He seemed to hesitate. "Now that it's safe for you to return to Texas."

She shook her head. "I have no plans to leave White-horse. At least not yet."

"You do know you can come to me if you need help." He said the words quietly. His gaze met hers.

"Thank you. I appreciate that."

Andi watched him drive away before she put on her coat again and left the office, locking the door behind her. The wind whipped at her Texas-climate clothing and she knew it was time she took Cade's advice.

Chapter Ten

Just as Cade was loading a few fishing supplies into his pickup, his brother pulled up in the patrol car.

Cade swore under his breath as Carter got out and walked toward him. A few more minutes and Carter would have missed him.

"I need to talk to you," Carter said in his cop voice.

Cade nodded and reached for his keys to open his apartment door. "What's up?" he asked, surprised how the snow had drifted around his back porch just in the time he was getting packed to go.

"When did you start locking your door?" Carter asked.

Cade didn't answer as he unlocked the door and stepped inside to flip on the light. It was one of those dark snowy days when the only good place to be was sitting in a fishing shack on the ice.

Opening the refrigerator, he took out two beers. He shot a look at Carter. "Isn't it your day off?" Carter grunted in response and Cade handed his brother a bottle. Carter took it reluctantly but didn't open it as

Cade screwed off the top of his and took a drink. He knew he was going to need it.

"What the hell, Cade?" Carter said, shaking his head at him.

Cade tilted his beer toward a chair in the small living room, dropping into one. He couldn't remember ever seeing his brother this angry and was betting Carter had run Starr Calhoun's name through the system as he'd requested. Once Carter saw a picture of Starr...

"I feel like running you in," Carter said.

Cade took a drink of his beer, watching his brother over the bottle.

With a curse, his brother twisted off the cap on his beer and sat down, tossing the cap onto the end table.

"First you say you want to know about Grace's parents," Carter said, biting off each word. "Which we both know was bull. You wanted to know if Grace Eden Browning existed, but I suspect you wouldn't have asked me to find out if you hadn't already known that no one by that name did."

Cade said nothing as his brother rushed on.

"Then you ask me to check out Miranda Blake, leading me to believe your interest in her was romantic." He hesitated but seeing that Cade wasn't going to comment continued. "Then you want to know about Starr Calhoun. When I ran the names I also requested photos. Why the hell didn't you tell me?"

Cade shook his head. "I was still trying to assimilate it myself."

"Grace was Starr Calhoun."

"So it appears," Cade said. "I couldn't come to you with this until I figured out some things for myself."

"The Lone Ranger," Carter said under his breath. "You've always been like this. Can't stand to ask for help. You're just like the old man."

Cade couldn't argue that.

"So what have you figured out?" Carter asked sarcastically.

Cade shook his head.

Carter glared at him for a long moment, then took a pull on his beer. He swallowed and put the bottle down on the table beside him. He pulled a thick file from inside his jacket and tossed it on the small coffee table between them.

"Starr Calhoun and her family of criminals."

Cade looked down at the file, but didn't pick it up.

"Why do I have the feeling that nothing in there is going to come as a surprise to you?" his brother asked.

Cade said nothing, waiting for Carter to run out of steam. He knew his brother. Carter needed to get everything off his chest, then they could talk.

Carter took another drink of his beer. "How long have you known that Grace was Starr Calhoun?" he asked more calmly.

"Not long." He'd been two steps behind on all of this from the time he'd seen Grace on the highway that summer day more than six years ago.

He wasn't equipped to handle any of it given the way he'd felt about her. Worse, his brother was right about him. He wasn't good at asking for help. But right now he wanted nothing more than to turn this all over to him. Carter was the sheriff. He would know what to do when Cade didn't. Mostly it would take it out of his hands.

"I've been behind the eight ball on this from the moment I met Grace...Starr," he corrected.

"Then you had no clue she wasn't who she said she was?"

"I knew something in her past was bothering her. I thought she was still in love with some man." He chuckled at his own foolishness.

Carter shook his head and took another drink of his beer as Cade told him about Miranda Blake showing up at his door with the photograph of Starr Calhoun. "I still have trouble believing it, let alone accepting it."

"I assume you know about the bank robberies."

Cade nodded. "And before you ask, I don't know anything about the money."

"Three million dollars," Carter said. "Never found. On top of that, one of Starr's brothers was released from prison about three weeks ago. He's broken his parole and no one knows where he is. He's considered dangerous. Name's Lubbock Calhoun."

His brother must have seen his expression. "So you know about that, too." Carter swore. "Then you know the connection between the Calhouns and Miranda Blake."

Cade frowned. Connection?

"Other than the fact that they were both from Texas, it turns out that Ms. Blake's father was killed in a bank robbery. He was gunned down by Amarillo Calhoun, the eldest son of the Calhouns. It's all in the file, including the fact Miranda Blake was there that day at the bank." He nodded at Cade's no doubt shocked expression. "It gets better. Both she and Starr Calhoun were there. They were both about five at the time."

Cade couldn't have spoken even if he'd wanted to. Andi and Starr. Hadn't he known there was more to the story?

"What does Miranda Blake want out of this?" Carter asked.

"The story," Cade said slowly, still stunned by the import of what his brother had told him.

"You don't think she might be looking for a little revenge?" Carter asked.

"For her father's death? I would imagine there's some of that, too."

"You don't really believe it's a coincidence that both Starr and Miranda ended up here, do you?" Carter asked.

Cade smiled ruefully. "Someone wanted her to uncover this story. They've been giving her information anonymously."

"And that doesn't worry you?" Carter snapped.

"Yeah, it worries me. Especially after what you just told me."

"Especially after whoever was at her apartment last night," Carter said. "Three million dollars. Men have killed for a lot less. And so have women."

"Andi isn't after the money," Cade said.

His brother raised a brow. "And you know that how?"

Cade glanced at the file on the coffee table, no longer sure of anything.

"There's something else in that file," Carter said. "It's about Houston Calhoun, the brother Starr allegedly robbed the banks with."

"I know he's been missing—"

"Not anymore," the sheriff said. "That body we found in the abandoned Cherry House down in Old Town a while back? Well, I finally got an ID on it. It was Houston Calhoun."

Cade took the news like a blow.

"We were able to identify the remains through DNA. He'd had his DNA taken the last time he did prison time."

Cade swore, knowing what was coming next.

"You still have that .45 Colt Dad gave you?" Carter asked.

"I haven't seen it for a while," Cade said, surprised how calm he sounded when his whole life was about to blow sky-high. "Why?"

"Because Houston Calhoun had a .45 slug embedded in his skull. That's right, big brother. Houston was murdered and you better hope to hell you can find that gun and it doesn't match the slug taken out of the back of your former wife's brother's skull."

"Stop looking at me like I'm a suspect," he said, more angry with himself than his brother. He'd gotten himself involved in this when he'd fallen for Starr Calhoun. Not just fallen for her, but married her and fathered their child. A woman he'd never really known.

"Did you ever meet her brother?" Carter asked, sounding more like the sheriff than his brother.

"No. I didn't even know she had a brother. She told me she was an only child."

"He would have been a threat to your life with her," Carter said. "Based on the way the body decomposed, the anthropologist at the crime lab says Houston Calhoun died before winter set in approximately six years ago."

Cade swore. "I didn't know who Starr was or that Houston Calhoun even existed. And I sure as hell didn't kill him."

"Someone did. Knowing what we do now, he probably came to get his share of the money."

Cade watched another chunk of his life with Grace wash away. Soon there wouldn't be anything left but the lies. He had to face the fact that she might have killed her brother—and possibly with Cade's own gun.

He told himself if she'd done it, she did it because Houston was threatening to expose her. She would have wanted to stay and have Cade's baby, to put that old life behind her, to protect him from her past.

"If Grace killed him, she'd only been defending herself." Cade just didn't want to believe it had been about the money.

"No way to ever prove that now," Carter said. "You should be more concerned about keeping yourself out of prison."

"Damn, Carter, I'm your brother. You really think I shot that man and hid his body in the old Cherry House?"

"No. But you have to admit given all the facts, including that the body was hidden in an old house that you and I used to play in when we were kids, makes you look damned suspicious."

Cade knew what his brother was saying. How had the killer known that the house was abandoned, boarded-up and marked with No Trespassing signs? Or that the house was considered haunted by most everyone in Old Town Whitehorse?

"You ever mention the place to Grace? Maybe even show it to her on your way out to see our old ranch?" Carter asked, then read his expression and swore. "Damn, Cade, this is one hell of a mess."

Andi had been right. He was up to his neck in this whether he liked it or not with little way out unless he could prove he didn't know Grace was Starr Calhoun.

And there was little chance of that.

AT THE MERCANTILE store, Andi told the clerk that she needed some Montana winter clothing.

The clerk laughed. "Did you have something in mind?"

"Whatever it takes for me to be warm."

Forty minutes later, Andi left the store carrying her business suit, leather coat and stylish boots in a large bag. She wore flannel-lined canvas pants, a cotton turtleneck, a wool sweater, a sheepskin-lined coat, heavy snowpacks on her feet and a thick knitted wool hat, leather mittens with wool liners and a knitted scarf.

She felt like a sumo wrestler, but she *was* finally warm. She smiled as she called the local automotive shop to see about getting a head-bolt heater for her car and whatever it would take to get it running.

Once she had her car, she went looking for Cade. She had to tell him the truth about last night. He was in this almost as deep as she was. He had to be careful.

At his bait and tackle shop, she found a note on his door: Gone Fishing!

Great. At the convenience store, she filled up with gas and asked where everyone fished.

"This time of year?" the clerk said. "The reservoir. Drive north. You can't miss it."

The clerk was right. About fifteen minutes out of town, Andi spotted the white, smooth surface of the reservoir wedged between the low hills, and realized this was where Cade had brought her, only she didn't recall how to get to his cabin.

She parked on the edge of the ice, debating what to do. She could see four-wheelers and pickups parked out on the ice beside a dozen or more fishing shacks spread along the reservoir, but she wasn't about to drive her car out there because she could also see places where the ice looked thin or had a break in it. One of those shacks was Cade's.

At the sound of a four-wheeler coming across the ice, she got out of her car and waved down the man driving.

"You can drive out on the ice, it's plenty solid," the fishermen said over the thump of the four-wheeler's engine.

Andi stared out at the frozen expanse. She could see places where the ice had buckled. There wasn't a chance she was going to drive out there. It had been frightening enough just driving out from town on the snow-packed highway even with the new tires the automotive shop had put on for her when they'd added the head-bolt heater for the engine to keep it warm.

As if seeing her hesitation, the fisherman added, "Or I could give you a ride." He motioned to the seat behind him on the four-wheeler.

At least a four-wheeler would be lighter than a car, and the man obviously knew where to go to avoid any thin ice. At least she hoped so.

"Thank you. I will take you up on your kind offer," she said.

"Best get your warmest clothing out of the car," he suggested.

She grabbed her hat, mittens and scarf from the car and waddled over to the four-wheeler to awkwardly climb on behind him. She would never get used to all this clothing.

He gave the four-wheeler gas and they sped off down the rocky shore bouncing along until they hit the ice of the reservoir.

They raced across the frozen expanse, the cold air making her eyes tear. She hung on for dear life expecting to hear the crack of the ice followed by the deadly cold splash of the frigid water.

After what seemed like forever, her driver slowed the four-wheeler, coming to a stop next to what looked like a large outhouse. To her surprise, she could see that it had a stovepipe and smoke was blowing horizontally across the gray sky the moment the wind caught it. Snow had been packed around the bottom of the shack except in front of the door.

"Cade," the man called. "You've got a visitor."

CADE WAS HALF-AFRAID it would be his brother with an arrest warrant.

The first thing Cade had done after talking to Carter back in town was head out to the cabin. He owned half a dozen guns that he kept in a safe in the back room of the cabin. He used to hunt with his father and he kept a .357 Magnum out for protection although he'd never had to use it for that.

Once inside the cabin, he'd gone right to the back bedroom, opened the closet and turned on the light so he could open the safe. It held twelve rifles. He had only three in it and a couple of shotguns along with the .45 his father had given him.

As he turned the dial, his fingers trembling as he tried to remember the combination, he recalled the day Grace had asked him what was in the safe.

"Guns."

She'd raised a brow and he'd laughed.

"You're in Montana. Practically everyone owns at least one, most a whole lot more than that. We still hunt in this state."

"Can I see them?" she'd asked.

"Sure. Have you ever shot a pistol?"

She'd shaken her head. "Could I?"

He recalled her excitement, his mouth going dry, his stomach roiling. Right away, she'd taken to shooting the .45 his father had given him.

"It looks like something one of the Old West outlaws would have used," she'd said.

He hadn't told Andi, but he was more than aware of

Grace's interest in outlaws. He'd thought of it more as an interest in the history of the area and he'd encouraged it, wanting her to feel about this place as he did.

He heard a click and reached for the safe's handle, half praying the .45 would be there and half hoping it wouldn't. Without the gun, Carter couldn't prove that the bullet that killed Houston Calhoun had come from Cade's pistol.

But the gun might also clear him—and Grace as well. He'd been praying that would be the case as he'd opened the safe door.

He'd had a bad feeling even before he opened the safe door that the .45 wouldn't be there.

If Grace shot her brother with it, then she would have gotten rid of the gun, right?

Or put the gun back where it would be found long after she was gone to incriminate Cade.

The gun wasn't where he usually kept it.

Panicked, he'd begun to search the other drawers, knowing he wasn't going to find it. He had sat down on the hardwood floor, sick at heart with what this meant. The only person who could have taken the gun was Grace. Starr, he reminded himself. There had been no Grace.

His heart had sunk with the realization that he hadn't known his wife at all. He'd trusted her. When he'd opened the safe that day to teach her how to use a gun, he'd let her see the combination—no doubt exactly why she'd asked him to teach her to shoot. He would bet Starr Calhoun and guns were no strangers to each other.

He'd gotten up from the floor, closed the safe door and called his brother with the bad news.

All Carter had done was swear. The loss of the .45 was a double-edged sword. Without the gun, Cade couldn't prove he was innocent of Houston Calhoun's murder. But with it, the gun might have seen him straight to prison.

As he'd left the cabin to go down to his fishing shack he was thankful at least that Starr hadn't put the gun back into the safe to frame him for murder.

Maybe there was a little Grace in her after all.

He'd gone fishing, just wanting to be left alone. And he had been until now.

ANDI WATCHED as a plywood door scraped open and Cade Jackson looked out. He appeared anything but pleased to see her as she swung off the four-wheeler, thanked the fisherman for the lift and waited for him to speed off again before she looked at Cade.

"Aren't you going to invite me in?" she asked when he said nothing.

Without answering he disappeared back inside, but left the door ajar. She moved across the glare of wind-scoured ice and stepped inside.

Being from Texas she'd never seen an ice-fishing house except on the movie *Grumpy Old Men.* This one was a lot like Cade's apartment—small and light on amenities.

"Watch your step," he said, moving around a large square hole in the ice to close the door behind her.

They were instantly pitched into darkness. The only light came from below her feet. The ice seemed to glow, the large hole cut into it like a wide-screen television.

She let out a cry of surprise as several fish crossed the open water in the hole and heard Cade's amused chuckle.

He pointed to a small folding stool. "Since you're here you might as well sit down."

He picked up what looked like a metal pitchfork and stood over the hole in the ice as fish passed beneath them.

"You don't use a fishing pole?" she asked.

He shook his head and motioned for her to be quiet.

Suddenly a large fish appeared. Cade moved so fast she almost missed it.

An instant later he drew the speared fish out of the water and grinned at her. "Hungry?"

"I need to tell you something," she said. "It's about the man who attacked me yesterday."

"Not on an empty stomach, okay?" He gave her a pleading grin.

She nodded, but as they left the fishing house she couldn't help but feel they were being watched.

Chapter Eleven

Arlene Evans was at the end of her rope by the time she reached the mental hospital. For days she'd done everything possible to discover the identity of the man who'd fathered Charlotte's baby.

Her daughter had observed her efforts with sly amusement. "You'll never find out because you wouldn't be able to guess in a million years."

And now Arlene had just spent hours in the car with her pregnant, obstinate daughter and her reticent son.

"Why do we have to go in?" Charlotte whined as Arlene Evans came around to the passenger side of the car, opened the door and ordered her adult children to get out.

"Your sister has asked for the three of us to come to Family Day and we didn't drive all this way for you not to go in," Arlene snapped. "Now get out and shut up."

Charlotte shot her a deadly look but climbed out of the car, making Arlene wonder how she could have missed the fact that her daughter was pregnant.

She flushed with shame as she watched her son slowly climb out of the back seat. He wore black combat boots, a tattered pair of jeans with huge holes in them, a T-shirt with obscenities scrawled across the front and a gray knitted-wool stocking cap, his dirty hair sticking out.

"Do you have to wear that hat?" she demanded.

He grunted and walked toward the gate into the mental hospital.

Arlene followed Bo and Charlotte, afraid there was even worse waiting inside for her.

THE ELDEST daughter of Arlene Evans watched from the third floor window, smiling to herself. The family had arrived. Bile rose in her throat. Violet Evans had looked forward to this day almost from the first.

Soon it would be all worth it. Soon she would walk out those doors and be a free woman. Excitement rippled through her, but she quickly squelched it.

She had to be very careful now and not overplay her hand. It would be difficult to be in the same room as her mother and not go for her throat. Not to mention let on her feelings toward her siblings.

But she had come this far using her brains and the drugs her brother had been able to sneak in for her.

She knew the picture she had to portray during Family Day. As long as she kept her true feelings hidden...

She laughed to herself. She'd been hiding her feelings since she was old enough to realize what a disappointment she was to her mother.

Violet hadn't known why her mother found her

lacking until she got older and heard some of the girls at school saying she was ugly.

She had looked into the mirror and seen a version of her own mother's face.

That's when she'd known the reason her mother hated her: her mother saw herself in her oldest daughter.

"Violet?"

She turned to see the nurse coming down the hall.

"It's time. Your family has arrived and they're anxiously waiting downstairs to see you."

Sure they were. Violet put on her timid, withdrawn look as she nodded and let the nurse lead her down to Family Day.

AFTER A SHORT WALK to his cabin, Cade filleted the fish, seasoned it and put the Northern Pike on the grill while Andi made a salad. He watched her out of the corner of his eye, her movements precise. He liked her hands. They were small, the fingers tapered, the nails a pale pink, the skin smooth as porcelain.

"What?" she asked and he realized she'd caught him staring at her.

"You make a nice salad."

She seemed to relax. She'd probably been as surprised as he was when he suggested they take the fish back to his cabin for lunch. He'd never thought he'd bring her back here.

"Mind setting the table?" he asked, getting down two plates, knowing she wouldn't.

He watched her for a moment, warmed by the heat

of the kitchen—and the closeness of another human being—before going back outside to the grill.

Lifting the lid on the charcoal grill, he turned the fish. Grace had suggested they get a stove with a grill so he wouldn't have to cook outside in the winter.

But he liked grilling when it was cold. Even when it was snowing as it was now. He liked seeing his breath mingle with the scent of the Northern Pike filets grilling just under the metal hood.

He felt his stomach rumble and tried to remember the last time he'd been this hungry. Most of the time he forgot to eat and then just cooked up something to keep himself going.

When the fish was ready, he went inside for a serving platter. Andi had set the table in front of the fire. The flames played off her face as she looked up at him. Her features softened and she smiled.

"How is it out there?" she asked. She'd been shocked that he planned to grill the fish outside in this kind of weather.

"It's ready. I hope you're hungry."

She nodded. "Starved."

He went back outside in the falling snow and cold and shut down the grill. With the fish filets on the serving plate he returned to the cabin to find her waiting by the door.

She took the plate from him. "Oh, it smells wonderful," she said as she carried it over to the table.

Cade knocked the snow from his coat and hat and slipped off his boots before joining her.

She had turned on the stereo. One of his Country and Western CDs was playing softly.

"I hope you don't mind," she said, obviously seeing his surprise. "This CD is one of my favorites."

He shook his head. It was also one of his favorites.

They ate listening to the music, neither saying much other than to compliment the food.

"Your first Northern Pike?" he asked.

She nodded. "It's good."

"So's the salad." They were being so polite to each other it was making him nervous. "Look," he said, putting down his fork. "There must be something you and I can talk about other than criminals, isn't there?"

She smiled. "Who knows? We've never tried."

He returned her smile and picked up his fork. "So let me guess, your favorite food is Tex-Mex."

She laughed. "How did you know?"

They spent the rest of the meal talking about food, music, television and books that they liked, bands they'd heard, places they wanted to visit.

After they finished eating, they cleared the dishes together. As he washed and she dried, she told him about what the attacker had said to her.

"I have some news, too," he said and told her about the talk he'd had with his brother—and about the missing .45.

ARLENE SQUIRMED in her chair as she heard footfalls coming down the hall. It had been months since she'd seen her daughter Violet. Not since the night her eldest daughter had tried to smother her with a pillow.

She didn't like to recall the events of last summer. All her near-death "accidents." Sometimes late at night when she couldn't sleep she would know that she had done a horrible disservice to Violet.

She hadn't wanted the child, hadn't wanted to be pregnant, certainly hadn't enjoyed lovemaking with Floyd. But as her mother said, beggars can't be choosers.

And that was how Arlene had gotten pregnant. In the backseat of a beat-up old sedan. Floyd had only agreed to marry her after her father had threatened him. They'd gone before a justice of the peace over in Choteau and come back to Whitehorse married.

While she was tied down with a squalling baby, Floyd escaped to the barn or the tractor out in a field or town for fertilizer.

Arlene had hated marriage, motherhood and the baby. She'd just been thankful that the day would come that she could marry Violet off.

And then along had come Bo almost ten years later and then Charlotte shortly after that. Both times only because Floyd had forced himself on her.

After that, she saw even less of Floyd, which suited them both fine. Until last summer when he'd left her for good.

Arlene watched the doorway for Violet, telling herself that it wasn't too late to make it up to her.

But then her daughter appeared in the doorway, stooped, lanky, dull brown hair, hollow eyed, resembling a kicked puppy, and Arlene knew that coming here had been a huge mistake.

ANDI COULDN'T BELIEVE Houston was dead. Murdered. "Your brother doesn't think you killed him."

"No. But I have to admit, I look guilty as hell," Cade said. "Not only was it my gun, but everyone knows how I felt about Grace. For the last six years I've mourned the loss of her and our baby. I would have done anything to protect Grace and our baby."

"Even kill?"

Cade looked away for a moment. "I didn't kill Houston in case you're wondering."

"I wasn't. I know you didn't kill anyone."

He turned back to look at her again. "You could be wrong about me."

She shook her head. "I'm a pretty good judge of character since I make a living telling other people's stories." She said nothing for a moment, then, "You don't seem all that surprised that Lubbock's after the money."

"I'm not. I've thought this was about the money since I found out about it. I just wasn't sure how *you* fit into it." He met her gaze. "Did you call 911 from your apartment?"

"No, just as I told your brother. I can't explain it. Unless Lubbock called right before he grabbed me. Maybe it was a test to see if I would tell your brother what he said."

"Unless there was someone else in your apartment and the whole thing was a setup," Cade said.

"You don't think I—"

He cut her off. "No. I was thinking more of Starr. If you're right and she's alive."

"Then that would mean that Houston hid the money and she and Lubbock don't know where."

He shrugged as he finished the dishes and drained the water in the sink, reaching for the end of her dish towel to dry his hands.

"Have you ever caught a fish through a hole in the ice?" he asked with an obvious change of subject.

"Do I have to spear it?"

He laughed. "No, you can use a hook and a line if you're squeamish."

"I'm not squeamish," she said.

He'd cocked a brow at her. "It's still light out if you'd like to go back down and fish for a while."

NEITHER ARLENE nor Bo nor Charlotte moved as Violet stepped tentatively into the room.

"What do you have to say to your daughter, Mrs. Evans?" the doctor said, an edge to his voice.

Arlene found her feet and, opening her arms, moved toward Violet. "How are you, dear?"

Violet cringed as her mother touched her.

"It's all right, Violet," the doctor said. "Please come in and join us." He got up to close the door.

Arlene felt his gaze as it swept from her to Charlotte to Bo. He was looking at the three of them as if they were the ones who needed psychiatric counseling.

Violet, her head down, her fingers picking nervously at the sacklike dress she wore, took a chair near the doctor. Arlene sat down again although what she really wanted was to flee. She should never have come here let alone brought Bo and Charlotte. This was all about blaming the family, making them feel bad.

"Violet, what is it like having your family here?" the doctor asked.

"Good."

"Isn't there something you want to say to them?" he asked.

Violet slowly raised her gaze to her mother. "Where's Daddy?"

Arlene winced. Daddy? Violet and her father had never been close. He'd avoided the child just as he had them all.

"Floyd left after what you did, Violet. I have no idea where he is," Arlene said, getting angrier by the moment.

"Oh," Violet said and dropped her gaze again.

"Is there something you'd like to say to your daughter, Mrs. Evans?" the doctor asked pointedly.

Violet raised her head. What could have been a smile played at her lips. Arlene looked into her daughter's eyes and winced at the carefully hidden hatred she saw there.

"No," she said. "There isn't."

The doctor looked shocked. He blinked then turned to Charlotte. She was playing with her hair and looking bored. "Perhaps you'd like to say something to your sister?"

"Do they make you wear those awful clothes?" Charlotte asked.

Violet let her gaze slide to her sister. She looked sad and embarrassed as she touched the worn fabric. "I didn't have any of my own clothes."

The doctor looked down at the notebook on his lap.

Arlene hadn't seen him take any notes. He seemed stunned by the lack of interaction between them.

"What about you?" he asked Bo. "Isn't there something you'd like to say to your sister?"

Bo also had a bored expression. Slouched in his chair, he scratched his neck for a moment and considered Violet.

"When are you getting out of here?" he asked.

Violet gave him a cheerless smile. "I don't know. When I'm well."

"You look…" Arlene couldn't finish. There was a lump in her throat. "Your sister is pregnant." The words just came out. She felt shame that they sounded like an accusation. But then everything had always been Violet's fault in one way or another.

Violet looked at Charlotte. "A baby? Oh, I'd love to see it when it's born." She looked hopefully at the doctor. "Do you think there's any chance…"

"We'll have to see," he said noncommittally. "You keep making improvements like you have…"

Arlene rose. "I'm glad you're getting well, Violet."

"Thank you, Mother," Violet said, lowering her head again.

"We should go," Arlene said.

"Violet, was there anything else you wanted to say?" the doctor prodded.

She nodded. "The doctors told me what I did." She raised her head. Huge tears welled in her eyes and slowly rolled down her cheeks as she looked at her mother. "I can't believe I would do such a thing. I'm so sorry. I just hope you can forgive me someday." Violet began to cry softly.

Arlene nodded and turned to give her two youngest an impatient look. They finally rose to leave.

"It was good seeing you, Violet," Charlotte said. "If my baby is a girl maybe I'll name her after you."

As Bo walked by Violet, he knelt down and took both her hands in his. "Take care, Vi." He rose again and walked out the door.

Arlene saw Violet palm something in her hand, then secretly slip it into her pocket.

Bo had given his sister something. A note? What?

Violet rose as Arlene started to move past her. Standing, she and her mother were about the same height. "Thank you for coming, Mother."

Arlene was still shocked by the hatred she'd seen in Violet's eyes earlier. Now that hatred was watered down with tears, but still shining brightly, leaving little doubt what Violet would do if she was ever released from here.

"My daughter isn't well," Arlene said to the doctor suddenly. "She has no business leaving here. Ever."

Violet seemed to crumble as she dropped into her chair and put her face in her hands.

"Really, Mrs. Evans," the doctor chided. "Violet was sick but now she is trying so hard to get well."

"You don't know her like I do," Arlene argued over the quietly weeping Violet curled up in her chair like a child. "All this is for show. She wants you to believe that *we're* the problem—not her, but it's not true. You can't let her out."

"That decision isn't up to you, Mrs. Evans," the doctor said sharply. "Violet is an adult. When she's well, she has a right to make a life for herself outside these walls."

"She's fooled you, but she hasn't me," Arlene said. "Look in her pocket. I saw her take something from her brother and put it in her pocket."

The doctor started to refuse but Arlene insisted.

"I'll show you how deceptive my daughter is, Doctor."

With apologies to Violet, he checked one pocket of her loose jumper, then the other.

"Her pockets are empty, Mrs. Evans," he said angrily. "Are there any more allegations you'd like to make before you leave?"

Violet raised her head just enough that Arlene could see the triumph in her eyes.

What had Violet done with whatever it was her brother had given her?

"I'm going to have to ask you to leave now, Mrs. Evans," the doctor said. "I won't have you upsetting my patient further. You will not be welcome here again."

"Don't worry," Arlene said. "I won't be back and I'll fight to keep Violet in here where she belongs. You can't let her come back to Whitehorse. Ever."

"Goodbye, Mother," Violet said, teary voice cracking.

Arlene stopped at the door but she didn't look back. "Goodbye, Violet." As she left, she prayed she'd never set eyes on her oldest daughter again.

Chapter Twelve

Andi couldn't remember a time she'd enjoyed more. For a while she forgot about everything and just enjoyed herself. This Cade Jackson was fun. They'd laughed a lot, spending most of their time in the ice-fishing house talking until it was too dark to see the fish any longer.

They walked back up to the cabin and she was surprised to see that Cade was armed. She hadn't seen him get the pistol before they'd gone down to the fishing shack. He must have had it hidden under his coat.

It reassured her. She'd thought he hadn't been taking any of this seriously. But the gun proved that he had. The man continued to surprise her.

A sliver of moon peeked out of the clouds and for once it wasn't snowing. The air was cold but walking next to Cade she felt more than toasty, the snow crunching under their feet. The night was bright enough that they could see for a great distance in this open country.

Andi realized she wasn't afraid with Cade. There was a strength about him, a determination that might even match her own. He understood the danger they were in, and she felt safe here with him.

Without looking at her, he said, "You've been through a lot with what happened to your father, the stalker in Texas and now this."

"I was in the public eye," she said, thinking about what Bradley had said. "Sometimes viewers think they know you. They would send presents or cards and letters. One time on the air I mentioned that my favorite flower was the daisy. I got dozens of daisies over the next few weeks. It's amazing also how much there was about me on the Internet."

"But you said the stalker turned out to be someone you worked with?"

She nodded. "A woman who wanted my job, I guess. She got her boyfriend to help her."

"The police didn't suspect her right away?" he asked.

"Apparently not." Andi frowned. "I still have a hard time believing it. I met her boyfriend once when she brought him down to the station to show him around. He seemed nice."

"She must have wanted your job awfully bad," he said. "It doesn't surprise me that she could talk her boyfriend into helping her. He probably loves her."

"Or did. They both deny it, but apparently the police found evidence that ties them both into the stalking." She sighed. "Anyway, it's over. Now I feel as if I panicked unnecessarily, leaping, as it is, from the skillet into the fire."

"And you're angry with yourself, right?"

She looked over. "Yes, how did you—"

"I've been doing a little running myself so I know the feeling." There was a smile in his voice.

"At least you were grieving for the death of the woman you loved," she said.

He chuckled softly, stopping at the top of the rise to turn to look back at the frozen reservoir. "That's what I told myself. But I think you and I know it was a little more complicated than that." He grew silent for a moment. She could hear the sound of the wind in the trees behind the dark outline of the cabin.

"You asked me the other day if I hadn't seen something that made me question my relationship with Grace," he said quietly.

She held her breath.

"They were such little things. Little doubts that nagged at me all these years even after she was gone." He looked over at her. "A part of me knew something was wrong. I could see her struggling sometimes." He chuckled. "I thought it was a man. The day I met her beside the highway changing her flat tire, I knew she had some past she was escaping from. I just assumed it was from a relationship. When I caught her looking anxious or worried, I told myself she was thinking about him."

Her heart went out to Cade. "I'm sorry it was so painful. I guess the truth wouldn't have been any easier, though."

He laughed and they started walking again toward the cabin. "No, the truth I'm afraid is going to get us both killed."

CADE DIDN'T ADD that being with a desirable woman again was also helping. He felt as if they were in the same boat. Both of their lives on the line. Both of them fighting the ghosts of their pasts.

It surprised him that he could feel that way about Andi Blake. Oh, desire, that was a given. Same with compassion for what she'd been through.

But at some point, he'd actually started liking her. A reporter. He never would have expected that in a million years.

"My car's on the other side of the lake," she said when they reached his front porch.

He nodded and looked back toward the reservoir. He could barely make out the shape of the fishing shack in the blackness of the winter night.

Across the lake, he could see multicolored Christmas lights glittering. He'd forgotten about Christmas, but in a few days he was expected at a party where his brother would be asking the woman he loved to marry him.

The clouds parted and a sliver of silver moon appeared, then dozens of tiny sparkling stars. Suddenly Cade felt very small in this huge universe. He looked up. A few more stars popped out of the clouds while tiny ice crystals sifted down from the cold blue of the sky.

The way he was feeling, he knew the smart thing was not to invite her in but to give her a ride to her car and go on back to his apartment tonight.

But he'd seldom, if ever, done the smart thing. He'd proved that by falling in love with Grace Browning.

Earlier he'd been glad to see that Andi had taken his

advice and gotten some warm Montana clothing. She was bundled up, a thick knitted cap pulled down over her dark hair. In the faint moonlight, he could see that her cheeks were flushed from the cold, her eyes sparking.

He reached over and grabbed a handful of the front of her coat and pulled her to him.

She stumbled into him, her eyes widening.

"There's something I've wanted to do since the first time I laid eyes on you," he said.

He cupped Andi's face in his gloved hands and pulled her into a kiss.

He felt her resist for an instant, tears welling in her eyes and then his lips touched hers. He felt a hot tear, tasted the salt. He pulled her into his arms, holding her tightly, telling himself he was in over his head.

But this felt right and for the first time in years, he wasn't afraid to feel. Her lips parted, her breath warm and sweet. He drew her closer, deepening the kiss.

Desire shot through him, heating his blood. He encircled her in his arms, pulling her as close as possible through all their winter clothing.

It wasn't close enough. He drew back from the kiss and realized he'd never wanted a woman the way he wanted this one. Not even Grace. He heard the soft intake of her breath as he pulled her toward him again, dropping his mouth to hers.

She answered in kind as he reached behind him and opened the door to the cabin.

In a flurry of clothing and kisses, they stripped off their coats and boots, hats and mittens, peeling off pants and sweaters as they stumbled locked together toward the couch.

The fire he'd made earlier before dinner had burned down to a few glowing embers, but they didn't need the heat. They were making their own.

Her skin felt on fire as he brushed his lips along her throat. He could feel her pulse quicken as he slipped his fingers beneath the thin fabric of her bra. Her nipples were hard and erect. She moaned as his fingers brushed over one then the other. He dropped his mouth to her warm breast, making her moan, and ran his hand over her flat, smooth, warm belly to slip into her panties.

She was hot and wet and pressing into him with a fierceness that matched his own. He looked into her eyes and saw that there would be no turning back for either of them as his fingers found her center.

ANDI ARCHED against him. From the moment Cade had pulled her to him on the porch, she knew she was a goner. She'd wanted him on a primal level that terrified and excited her. There was no thought, only the feel of him and the fire that shot through her straight to her core.

His fingers filled her as his mouth came back to hers. She could feel herself rising higher and higher, the pleasure building in intensity until she thought she couldn't take another instant. His skin was like a flame against hers, stoking the fire inside her. She could feel it building and building and suddenly she was bursting beneath him.

She gasped and cried out, her head thrown back,

pleasure coursing through her veins. She barely felt him remove her bra, then slip her panties down her legs. She lay naked on the leather couch, him above her.

In his dark eyes, she saw raw need flash like a hot spark ready to catch fire. It fanned her own longing as he stood and took off his pants and dropped his boxers to the floor.

With an abandon she never knew she possessed, she surrendered to him completely as inside the cabin, they made love through the night completely unaware that outside it had begun to snow again.

THE NEXT MORNING, Cade left Andi sleeping in the cabin and went outside.

From the cabin he had a good view of the area. He checked the trees behind the cabin and the arena first, looking for fresh tracks in the snow. There were none.

As far as he could tell no one had been around during the night. The news flooded him with relief.

Yesterday he'd thrown caution to the wind, feeling as if he'd been playing Russian roulette. He'd gone fishing when he should have been worrying about the Calhouns and his future. And even crazier, he'd curled up with Andi, making love all night, when they both were in danger.

Not that he regretted either. The memory of their lovemaking warmed him on the cold, snowy morning.

This morning, though, he couldn't keep pretending this mess was going to just go away. He knew what he had to do to save himself and Andi. They were in it together now and no matter what she said, he'd gotten her into it. He was the one who'd married Starr Calhoun.

As he walked down to the ice-fishing shack watching for tracks coming up from the reservoir, he thought of the outlaw books Grace had loved. She'd reveled in this part of Montana's past. The Curry brothers, Butch Cassidy and the Sundance Kid and many more had made this area home for a while.

Some of them were so much a part of the community that area ranchers would hide them from posses and even lie on the stand for them. Not that some didn't fear them and the repercussions if they hadn't.

As he walked, the fresh snow crunched under his boots and his breath in the cold morning air came out in frosty white puffs. It was early enough that he didn't see any other fishermen down by the lake. He liked the utter silence of winter mornings. It was his favorite time.

And this morning he really needed the time to get himself together before he saw Andi. They needed a plan. There were decisions to me made. Lubbock, or whoever had attacked her, would be back. Cade didn't doubt that for a moment.

How the hell they were going to find the missing money, he had no idea. But they had to at least make the attempt because if he was right, someone had been watching them for several days now.

He could hear the ice cracking closer to shore, but he wasn't worried. The ice was thick and would be for months.

He couldn't help but think about yesterday with

Andi. He'd had fun. That surprised him. She'd let down her defenses and he had, too. Maybe that's why their lovemaking had been like none he'd ever experienced. He got the impression that she'd been so busy building her career that she hadn't dated much—let alone gotten close to a man.

As he neared his ice fishing shack, he slowed. The wind had blown long into the night, but he could still make out the slight indentations in the snow on the lea side of the shack that had once been footprints.

The house was covered with frost. The wind had drifted the new snow up one side of the wall and left the surface of the reservoir perfectly smooth and untracked except where someone had stood.

He pulled the .357 Magnum from under his coat and stepped as quietly as possible to the door. As he cautiously pulled it open, the breeze caught the door and threw it back. He jumped back and the door banged against the side of the shack and stayed there. Then everything was deathly silent again.

No sound came from inside. Cade waited a few more seconds before he carefully peered around the edge of the door.

The first thing that hit him was the scent. The ice was an aquamarine-green—except where he'd cut the large rectangular hole. Yesterday there had been open water in the hole but during the night it had iced over.

There was something dark smeared along the edge of the thicker ice next to the iced-over hole that made his mouth go dry. He'd smelled enough dead animals as a ranch boy to recognize it as blood.

His pulse drummed in his ears so loudly he almost didn't hear the approaching crunch of boot soles on the new snow. The steps were slow, tentative.

He flattened himself to the side of the shack, the gun ready, but not knowing which side of the shack the person would come around.

"Cade?" Andi said as she appeared to his right by the open door of the fishing shack. She looked from his face to the gun in his hand.

"Stay back," he snapped as he stepped to the doorway to shield her.

But she'd already looked in and no doubt seen the smear of blood on the ice. Her eyes widened and a gasp escaped her lips. As she stumbled back, one gloved hand over her mouth, he turned to see movement beneath the ice.

Only this time it wasn't fish.

A face appeared beneath the ice. The skin was drawn and blue, the mouth open as if gulping for breath, the pale blue eyes staring blankly up from the freezing water.

ANDI COULDN'T get warm. She stood in front of the fire Cade had built before his brother had asked him to wait outside in the patrol car.

She rubbed her hands together and looked down into the flames. The sheriff had taken her statement and now stood next to her, making notations in his notebook.

"Where were you last night?" he asked.

"Here. All night."

He looked up from his notebook. "Can anyone verify that?"

"Cade."

He studied her for a long moment then wrote something down in the notebook. He'd already made it perfectly clear that he didn't approve of her—especially her and Cade. She wanted to assure him that she would never hurt his brother, but the truth was, she already had and she had no way of knowing what the future held any more than Cade or the sheriff did.

"Have you ever seen the deceased before?"

"No." Although she suspected she knew who he was.

"You have any idea why he was killed?"

"No."

"You don't think it might have something to do with why you're in Whitehorse?"

"I came here for a job."

"Right. You just happened to stumble across the fact that Grace Jackson was really Starr Calhoun."

"I didn't bring the Calhouns to Montana."

He nodded solemnly. "But you're up to your neck in this."

"I'm a reporter. I go after stories. I don't expect you to believe this, but someone got me involved in this—not the other way around."

He looked skeptical, just as she'd known he would. "I don't want to see my brother hurt."

"It's a little too late for that."

"I wasn't talking about Starr Calhoun," he said,

glancing toward the front window. "He's vulnerable. You're the first woman since Starr. Add to that he feels responsible for what's happening."

She wanted to argue that none of this was her fault, but she knew that wasn't necessarily true.

"When this is over, you'll make headlines again," the sheriff said. "You'll go back to your old job or get offered an even better television job in some big city. Cade won't ever leave Montana. If you think he will, then you don't know him. And even if you were able to get him to leave, well, a big city would kill him. He's a cowboy. He has to have room. This is his home."

She said nothing as he rose from his chair.

He looked as if there was more he wanted to say, but after a moment he turned and left.

When she heard the door close, she walked to the window and peeked out from behind the curtains. Cade was standing by the patrol car. He got in as Carter went around to the driver's side.

Andi turned from the window and stepped over to the fire again, chilled. She knew that Cade had recognized the resemblance between his deceased wife and the man under the ice. It was a Calhoun. It had to be Lubbock since Cade had told her that some remains found down in Old Town had turned out to be those of Houston Calhoun—and according to the crime lab, he'd been there about six years.

If the body was Lubbock Calhoun's, which she suspected, then she had to ask herself: Who killed him?

She felt another chill.

What if Starr really had faked her death and was not only alive, but back in Whitehorse?

CADE WATCHED a herd of antelope race across a wind-scoured snowy hillside just beyond the cabin as his brother started the patrol car and turned on the heater. The heater blew cold air, but not nearly as cold as Cade felt.

His brother was too calm, too much a cop on a case, and Cade knew he was in bad trouble.

"Any idea what a dead man was doing in your fishing shack?" Carter asked after a moment, pulling out his notebook and pen.

"I wish I knew."

"Where were you last night?"

Cade looked over at his brother. "In the cabin with Andi."

Carter swore. "We have an ID on the dead man from some jailhouse tattoos that we knew of from the APB out on him. His name is Lubbock Calhoun."

Cade nodded. No surprise there. He'd known the man was a Calhoun from his resemblance to his sister. Lubbock would have been his first guess since they'd known he had broken parole after getting out of prison.

"Had you ever seen him before?" Carter asked, writing down his responses.

"No."

"You have any idea who might have killed him?"

"None."

"When was the last time you used your fishing spear?"

"Yesterday."

"It appears he was killed with your spear," Carter said. "What are the chances the only prints on it will be yours?"

"I'd say pretty darned good."

His brother shook his head. "This all started with that damned reporter."

"Don't blame her. It actually started with Starr."

Carter put his notebook and pen away. "You're sure Ms. Blake didn't slip out last night while you were sleeping?"

He met his brother's gaze. "I didn't get much sleep last night so yes, I'm sure."

Carter swore. "Glad to see you took my advice and haven't gotten involved with her."

"I know you think I have lousy luck with women," Cade said. "But I loved Grace. Starr *was* Grace, a woman who wanted our baby, wanted this life with me and wanted to put all the rest behind her. I believe that with all my heart. Who knows how this would have ended if she hadn't died?"

Carter shook his head. "You're kiddin' yourself, bro. As long as that robbery money was missing, you and Starr, Grace, whatever, wouldn't have had a chance in hell. The only reason you haven't heard anything from this family is that Lubbock was locked up and Houston was dead. Now you've got a dead man in your fishing shack and I'm willing to bet he didn't break parole to come up here to ice fish."

"No, I think he was looking for the money. But apparently he's not the only one." Cade thought of Andi's theory about Starr. "What if Starr killed him?"

Carter shot him a look. "Starr's dead."

Cade realized it had always been coming to this. He had to know if that was her he'd buried. Or if everything he'd believed about his wife had been a lie. Otherwise, he knew he would never be able to put her to rest. "What would it take to have her body exhumed?"

"What?" Carter demanded. "You think she's *alive?*"

"I need proof that the woman who died in that car wreck was my wife. Andi thinks Starr might have faked her death and taken off with the money. Under the circumstances, I think we should know who all the players are, don't you?"

His brother looked at him. "You knew her. You can't really believe that your wife could kill someone in cold blood with a fishing spear?"

"Not the woman I married, no," Cade said. "But I think Starr Calhoun might have been more than capable of murder. My .45 is missing and Houston Calhoun is dead. Not to mention the body found in her car—if she faked her death."

Carter shook his head. "Well, at least now we have two of her brothers' DNA to compare hers to. If it's not Starr, we'll know soon enough."

Chapter Thirteen

"It was Lubbock, wasn't it?" Andi said as Cade entered the cabin.

He nodded. "Carter ID'd him from some prison tattoos." He stepped to her, taking her in his arms. "Are you all right?"

She nodded against his shoulder, burrowing into him. The fabric of his coat smelled of the outdoors and the cold but the feel of his arms around her warmed her to her toes.

"My brother upset you." He swore as he stepped back to look into her face, holding her at arm's length. "I should never have let him talk to you alone."

She smiled at that. "Like you could have stopped him. This is a murder investigation. He's worried about you."

Cade let out a laugh. "I'm worried about me."

"If it wasn't Lubbock who got me here, then who?" she asked.

He shook his head. "We've known all along that

whoever was behind this wanted the money. Someone must think I know where it's hidden."

"But who? If Lubbock was the one who was sending me the information and attacked me, then who killed him?"

Cade looked into her eyes. "I've asked my brother to see about getting Starr's body exhumed."

She stared at him. "Are you sure?"

"We have to know. If she's alive, then…" He couldn't finish at just the thought that the woman he'd loved and married was a killer.

ANDI SHUDDERED at the thought that Starr Calhoun was alive—and killing off the competition. "If she hid the money, then why wouldn't she just take it and leave?"

He shrugged. "Maybe there's more to it than money. Or maybe she can't find the spot where she hid it. Everything looks different in the winter. There's also the possibility that Houston hid it."

Andi thought about what Bradley had said. "Wouldn't whoever hid it have made some sort of map? Or at least written down the directions?"

Cade moved to the bookshelves with the outlaw books. "Grace did some drawings… I think they were in the back of one of these books. She was always sketching. She had talent as an artist."

"I can see that in her photographs," Andi said.

He glanced back at her with a grateful look that did more than warm her toes. "I still believe she wanted to be Grace."

"I think you're right." She stepped to him and put a hand on his arm. "That photograph of you in your bedroom… She loved you."

He looked away. "Here," he said, handing her a few books. "Let's see if there is some sort of map in here."

They spent the next few hours going through Grace's books. Many of them were inscribed to her from Cade with love. While there were small drawings often in the margins or notes, none of them appeared to be a map or diagram or clue to the missing money.

When they'd gone through her last book, Cade got up from the floor. "Well, that was a dead end."

Andi was just as discouraged. Why had she been given the article about Kid Curry? There had to be some connection. "I need to go to the newspaper. There might be another manila envelope waiting for me."

"I'm worried about you," Cade said. "It's not safe."

She smiled and leaned in to brush a kiss over his lips. "I'll be all right. It's Whitehorse. No one will grab me in the middle of Central Avenue. And anyway, whoever is behind this wants us to find the money. Until we do, I'm pretty sure we'll be safe."

"I hope you're right about that. I'll drive you to your car. I want to do some looking around the apartment. I'll call you if I find anything." He stepped to her, cupping her face in his hands. "Be careful. And please don't go back to your place. Stay with me at the apartment in town."

She nodded. There was no place she wanted to be other than with him right now.

He followed her into town, driving on past as she pulled into the diagonal parking in front of the newspaper building.

Getting out she fought that feeling again that she was being watched as she entered the building.

Her desk had numerous envelopes on it. She dug through, hoping for another manila envelope. At this point, she had no idea what to do next and could use all the help she could get.

But there was no manila envelope.

She did what she had to do at the paper, all the time thinking that she'd missed something at the museum.

Glancing at her watch she saw that it was still open if she hurried.

She went straight to the outlaw exhibit and, starting at the top left, studied each photo, each story. She had to have missed something.

She hadn't heard the elderly volunteer until the woman spoke, "We're closing in fifteen minutes, but you're welcome to stay until then."

"Thank you," Andi said, then noticed something she hadn't seen before. "What is that?" she pointed to a series of numbers and letters at the bottom of one of the exhibit cards, wondering if it referred to another exhibit.

"That's a geocaching site," the woman said.

"Oh, the game you play with a GPS."

"Don't let a hard-core geocacher hear you say that. They take it very seriously. There are two sites in our area. When you find the spot, you look for a container of some kind. Inside can be anything from a coin to a toy or a book to a map."

A map? Her heart began to pound. Bradley had said Starr would have had to have some way to find the money again. Like a global positioning system coordinate?

All she needed to find out was whether or not Cade had a GPS. It was too much to hope for.

But even if Cade had a GPS device, Starr wouldn't have been foolish enough to leave the site on it. She would have hidden the coordinates.

As the volunteers locked up the museum behind her, Andi glanced at her watch. It wasn't even four-thirty and it was already almost dark. She could feel the chill in the air as she called Cade's cell, too excited to wait until she got back to his apartment at the bait shop.

Starr Calhoun probably wouldn't have known about geocaching since it wasn't even started until 2000—just a year before she died.

But she could definitely have known how to use a GPS, especially if Cade had one. A lot of hunters and fishermen used them.

The phone rang four times before voice mail picked up. Disappointed, she started to hang up, then changed her mind and left a message telling him what she'd learned at the museum.

"If Starr had access to a GPS, then she might have left behind the coordinates to find the money, but for some reason hasn't been able to get to them. Call me." She snapped shut her phone, wondering where he was.

It was full dark now, the temperature dropping rapidly. Christmas lights tinkled on the houses around the museum and carols played on her car radio. She turned up the radio as she drove, surprised that the songs made her teary-eyed. She'd missed Christmas.

Up here in this part of Montana Christmas seemed so much more real than it had in Fort Worth. The snow helped considerably. But it was more than that.

It was Cade, she thought. She was falling for him. The thought sent a jolt of panic through her. She'd worked too hard at her career to fall for any man, especially one who lived in Whitehorse, Montana.

His brother was right. How could she stay here and continue her career? And she couldn't imagine Cade Jackson anywhere but here.

A part of her wanted to just keep going. Get on Highway 191 and head south until she hit Texas. But the rest of her couldn't wait to see Cade, couldn't wait to be wrapped in his arms, as she turned into the bait shop.

Her headlights flashed across the empty spot where he parked his pickup and she was filled with disappointment. She climbed out of her car and walked to the back of the building, her spirits buoying a little when she saw that there was a note on the back door.

The back door was unlocked. She reached inside to snap on the light, stepping in to read the note. A key fell out of the envelope. She picked it up and saw that it appeared to be a key to the apartment.

Andi,

I thought of a place Starr might have hidden the money. I'm driving up there. Stay here. There's a frozen pizza in the freezer. I'll be back as soon as possible.
Cade

She smiled at this thoughtfulness as she closed and locked the back door. The apartment felt cold. She kicked up the heat as she moved through it, taking off her coat. It felt strange being here without Cade.

As she neared the door to the bait and tackle shop, she noticed the thin line of light under the door.

Had a light been left on?

Even stranger, she thought, was that she felt a breeze. Almost as if the front door had been left open.

She hung up her coat and opened the door into the shop. She was hit with a wall of cold air. As she listened, she could hear the front door of the shop banging in the wind.

A faint light glowed near the front. She hurried down the narrow aisle, fishing items stacked almost to the ceiling, anxious to get the door closed.

The temperature was supposed to drop to more than twenty below zero tonight. She hoped nothing in the shop had been ruined because of the door being left open.

At the front door, she reached out and grabbed the achingly cold handle. She had to pull with all her strength to get it closed, the wind was so strong, and snow had drifted in, making it even more difficult.

The door finally slammed with a thunderous bang. She locked it and used the dead bolt as well, wondering how it could have gotten left open. Cade, no doubt, had other things on his mind.

She was halfway back down the aisle, when she noticed that the door to the apartment was closed. Strange, since she was sure she'd left it open. She'd almost convinced herself it had been the wind, when the small light at the front of the shop went out, pitching her into blackness.

CADE JACKSON had driven up into the Bear Paw mountains to the west of Whitehorse. He and Grace had picnicked there early in the fall among the ponderosa pines along a small creek.

She had been so happy that day. They'd eaten fried chicken, potato salad and fried apple pies that she'd made early that morning.

He'd been surprised how good a cook she was. They'd made love in the shade and fallen asleep.

He'd awoken to find the sun behind the trees and Grace gone.

She'd come hiking up thirty minutes later, after he called for her and hadn't gotten an answer. He had been getting worried something had happened to her.

She'd been apologetic, saying she'd just wanted to take a little walk and had been so taken with the country she'd lost track of how far she'd gone.

He'd thought it a wonder she hadn't gotten lost and said as much.

She'd told him she had a great sense of direction.

The Bear Paws were iced with snow this time of year. The picnic spot looked nothing as it had with ice covering the creek and the boughs of the pines heavy and white with the new snowfall.

He hiked in the way Grace had come out but he'd found no spot that looked like a great hiding place for three million dollars.

It was dark by the time he headed back to White-horse. As soon as he could get cell service, he called Andi. The call went straight to voice mail. She must have her phone turned off.

That was odd. He glanced at his watch. She should have been to the apartment by now.

That's when he noticed that he had a message. With relief he saw that it was from Andi.

He listened to it as he drove toward home, anxious to see her. Returning to the picnic spot had brought back a lot of memories—as well as doubts about Grace. How could he not have seen how secretive she was back then?

He knew he hadn't seen it for the very reason he hadn't wanted to. He'd wanted to believe she was exactly who she pretended to be.

"Geocaching?" he said and played the message a second time, realizing he'd missed something.

He listened again, then snapped the phone shut. "Sorry, Andi, it was a great idea, but I don't have a GPS," he said to the empty pickup.

But maybe Grace had one. No, not Grace, Starr.

There was no Grace. The only way she could be more dead to him was if Starr was alive and he found himself coming face-to-face with her.

He turned on the radio, trying to exorcise the memories and not worry about Andi. Christmas carols. It was only a few days until Christmas and he hadn't even shopped.

Not that he'd shopped the last six years, but this year he'd been starting to look forward to it.

As he saw the lights of Whitehorse appear on the dark horizon, he felt his excitement growing. He couldn't wait to see Andi. He just hoped her car would be parked behind the shop and the lights on in the apartment. Hopefully, too, she'd cooked the pizza because he was starved.

But as he pulled in, he saw that the parking space at the back was empty. No light on in the shop. No Andi.

He felt a sliver of worry burrow under his skin as he parked and got out. The note was gone off the back door. That made him feel better.

She'd at least been here. He turned on the light. There was no smell of store-bought pizza. He closed the door behind him, sensing something wrong.

The door to the shop was standing open. The light he always left on was out and there seemed to be a cold draft coming from the darkness.

Without taking off his coat, he moved toward the shop. The moment he was out of the light of his apartment, he drew the .357 and slipped into the darkness just inside the door to let his eyes adjust before he reached for the overhead light switch.

The florescent lights came on in a blink, illuminating the whole place. He moved swiftly to the farthest aisle where he could see the front door.

It was open. He remembered locking that door. It wasn't something he would forget.

Quickly he moved to the next aisle. Empty. Then the next. His heart dropped at the sight of the pile of spilled lures, the packages spread across the floor as if there'd been a struggle.

He rushed up the aisle and around the end to the counter. Nothing looked out of place—just as he'd feared. He hadn't been robbed. He'd known that the moment he'd seen that the big ticket items hadn't been taken—nor the cash register broken into.

At the front door, he peered out into the darkness. There were tracks in the snow, but the wind had filled them in except for slight hollows. He had no way of gauging how long ago the tracks had been made or by whom.

He slammed the door and bolted it, his heart in his throat. Where was Andi?

The phone rang, making him jump. He stared at the landline on the counter for a moment as he tried to calm down. It could just be a call asking if he had any minnows or if the fish were biting on Nelson.

But as he picked it up, he knew better.

Never in this world, though, did he expect to hear the voice he heard on the line.

His dead wife said, "Okay, now listen. You do as I say and we're all going to come out of this just fine."

"Grace?"

She didn't seem to hear, her voice clipped. "Do not go to the police. I've left my demands."

"Grace!" But she'd already hung up.

His hands were shaking so hard he had trouble putting the phone back into the cradle. He dropped to the stool behind the counter and tried to pull himself together.

Grace was alive. What about their baby? The child would be five years old.

He let out a sound, half sob, half choked-off howl.

This wasn't happening. It wasn't possible and yet he'd heard her voice. At first she'd sounded like her old self, then her words had become so unemotional. But it had been her.

Not Grace, he reminded himself. *Starr Calhoun* was alive.

And she had Andi.

He reached for the phone and checked caller ID. Blocked. He dialed *69. The phone rang and rang. No voice mail. Probably a cell phone that couldn't be traced.

He started to dial the sheriff's department, but stopped himself. Hanging up the phone, he remembered what she'd said. *I've left my demands.* He hurried through the shop back to the apartment and looked around, not seeing the manila envelope at first.

The envelope was propped against something in the corner of the counter. As he reached for it, he saw what had been behind the paper. Andi's shoulder bag with her new can of pepper spray. He'd seen it last night at the cabin and been thankful she had replaced the other can.

He'd known Andi had been taken when he'd seen the lures and realized there'd been a struggle. But seeing her shoulder bag brought it all home. Her car, though, hadn't been parked outside. He glanced in the purse, knowing her car keys would be gone. They were.

All his instincts told him to call Carter. As sheriff, Carter could put an APB out on Andi's car. Starr could be apprehended quickly—before she could do anything to Andi. But what if he jeopardized Andi's life? And what if Starr had kept the child, had the child with her?

He looked down at the large manila envelope still clutched in his left hand. *Do not go to the police.* Starr hadn't said anything about the sheriff. She knew his brother was the sheriff. Did it mean anything that she'd said police?

Semantics. He understood what she'd meant. He couldn't risk Andi's life. Houston was dead. Murdered. Lubbock was dead. Also murdered. Starr wasn't bluffing. She had nothing to lose. What was another murder?

Carefully he opened the envelope.

The words had been cut from a magazine so it resembled a kidnapping demand. Which was exactly what it was, he realized.

You have twenty-four hours.
Or your precious reporter dies.
Find the money.

I will contact you this time tomorrow.
Don't let me down.

His mind raced. Starr. But if she'd hidden the money, then she would know where it was. And if Houston had hidden it...

This didn't make any sense. Why would Starr think he knew where the money was? He remembered Andi asking the same question. Only then they'd believed it had been Lubbock who thought Andi could find it.

He began to pace the floor, trying to put it together. Lubbock hadn't known where the money was. Houston was dead. And now Starr didn't seem to know where the money was, either? Who the hell had hidden it then?

Geocaching. He thought back to Andi's message. But he hadn't had a GPS. He'd since purchased one, but he wasn't very good at using it. Had Starr had a GPS he didn't know about and used it to hide the money and now lost the coordinates?

Twenty-four hours. He swore. How was he going to find the money in that length of time when apparently the Calhouns couldn't find it?

Calm down. Starr thinks you know something, remember something. He jumped as his cell phone rang.

With trembling fingers he dug it out. "Hello?"

"Cade?" It was his brother.

"Carter, hey."

"Did I catch you in the middle of something? You sound...odd."

"As a matter of fact…" Cade said.

"Then I'll make this short and sweet. I got the judge to approve an emergency exhumation. I had to go out on a limb to get this. I've also got the crime lab standing by to run the DNA. Everyone is grousing about the added expense since the ground had to be heated. You do realize it's almost Christmas and colder than hell. But by tomorrow, we'll have our answer."

Cade wanted to tell him not to bother. He already had *his* answer. But he couldn't do that without risking everything. He cleared his throat. "Thanks."

"This is going to be over soon," Carter said.

That's what Cade feared.

Chapter Fourteen

In the wee hours of the morning, Cade sat bolt upright in his chair in the small apartment living room where he'd spent the night.

Daylight bled through the blinds. He hadn't slept more than a few minutes at a time, waking up with a start, everything coming back in a nauseating rush.

His head hurt, mind still reeling. But as he got up, he hung on to his waking thought.

Houston's body had been found down in Old Town, the original Whitehorse. The town had moved five miles north when the railroad came through to be closer to the line.

Assuming Starr had killed Houston, what was she doing in Old Town? There was little left in the old homestead town. A community center that served as the church and the home of the Whitehorse Sewing Circle famous for its quilts.

There were a half dozen houses, even more old foundations filled with weeds. Most of the population lived on ranches in the miles around Old Town.

The house where Houston's body had been found was known as the old Cherry House. Every kid in the county knew the place was haunted. Hell, Old Town had every reason to be haunted given everything that had happened out there over the years.

Most residents had seen lights not only in the abandoned, boarded-up Cherry House, but also in the old Whitehorse Cemetery. Along with lights, there'd been rumors handed down over the years of the eerie sound of babies crying late into the night.

Cade and his brother had played in the old Cherry House when they were kids even though every kid was told the house was dangerous and to stay out of it. Which only made him and Carter more anxious to go into the house.

He'd taken Starr to Old Town, past it to the ranch his family used to own, and he'd probably mentioned the place.

But still, how would she have gotten Houston into that house to kill him? There wasn't any way she could have carried his body down to the root cellar where his remains were found.

Unless he'd been alive when he'd gone down there. Unless she'd told him that's where she'd hidden the money.

Cade put call forwarding from the landline in the shop to his cell phone just in case Starr called again, then grabbed his coat and headed for the door. The sun on the new snow was blinding as he drove south. This time of the morning there was not another pickup on the road. He passed a couple of ranch houses, then there was nothing but the land, rolling hills that flattened as it fell toward the Missouri River Breaks.

He knew he was on a fool's errand. His brother and the rest of the sheriff's department had searched the entire house after getting an anonymous tip that there was a body buried in the house. The tip said the body was that of a woman who'd been missing for over thirty years.

As it turned out, the human remains were male and had only been in the ground not nearly as long.

Old Town looked like a ghost town as Cade drove past the community center, the cemetery up on the hill above town and turned down by the few houses still occupied to pull behind the Cherry House. He parked his pickup, hoping it wouldn't be noticed. The last thing he needed was to have some well-meaning resident call the sheriff.

Carter's men had boarded up the house again and put up No Trespassing signs. There'd been talk of burning the old place down since the county had taken it over for taxes and had had no luck selling it.

With a crowbar from his toolbox in the back of the truck, he pried up the plywood covering the back entrance enough that he could squeeze through. The job had gone much easier than he'd expected. Apparently he wasn't the first to enter the house since it had been reboarded up.

He was glad he'd brought the .357 under his coat since he wasn't sure who'd been here before him. Starr? Had she come back to the scene of the crime? It still bothered him. If she'd hidden the money, then why would she want him to find it? He had a hard time believing she couldn't find it again. She'd been nothing if not meticulous.

The house was cold, dark and dank inside. It smelled like rotting dead animals. He breathed through his mouth, waiting for his eyes to adjust to the darkness. The floor was littered with old clothing and newspapers.

Houston Calhoun wasn't the first person to die in this house. As the story went, one night more than thirty years ago, old man Cherry took his wife down to the root cellar, a dirt part of the basement where they kept canned goods, and shot her to death before blowing out his own brains.

To this day, no one knew why. The Cherrys left a son who died only weeks later in a car accident between Old Town and Whitehorse. The son left behind a wife, Geneva Cavanaugh Cherry, and two small children, Laney and Laci.

It was said that Geneva couldn't live with the death of her husband and took off never to be seen again.

Laney and Laci had been adopted by their grandparents, Titus and Pearl Cavanaugh and both had recently returned to Old Town after years away.

So it was no wonder that people believed the house was haunted, Cade thought as he snapped on his flashlight. He had no idea what he was looking for. Something. Anything that would give him a way to save Andi.

For years he'd believed he would never get over Grace—let alone ever fall in love again.

But the first time he'd laid eyes on Andi Blake he'd felt more than desire. He'd felt a strange pull.

It had been push-pull ever since. He'd fought it with all the strength he could muster. But he'd finally given up.

He knew he would be a fool to fall in love with her for a half dozen good reasons.

But he also knew reason flew out the window when it came to love. Grace had certainly proved that. He'd known she was running from something—just as he'd known Andi Blake was. But we were all running from something, haunted by our own personal demons, he thought as he searched the ground floor before climbing the rickety stairs to the floor above.

There was less debris up here. A couple of old bed frames and mattresses that the mice had made nests in. A few old clothes that had faded into rotten rags.

He shined his flashlight on the walls. Someone had used spray paint to write obscenities on several of the walls. He moved through, stopping at a small bedroom off the back. It was painted a pale yellow. Grace's favorite color.

With the flashlight, he swept the beam across the room. His hand stopped as something registered. He sent the beam back until he saw where someone had written some words in a neat black script.

Like a sleepwalker, he stepped into the room, the beam illuminating on a couple of the words. His heart began to beat harder, his breath coming in painful puffs, the room suddenly chilling.

Only you know my heart.
Only you know my soul.
Find me for I am lost.

He shuddered as if an icy hand had dropped to his shoulder. The cold seemed to permeate the room.

Grace's meticulous handwriting. He would know it anywhere.

He closed his eyes. How long had this been there? This cry for help? He backed into a wall and leaned there, wanting to howl, his pain was so great.

He *had* known her.

But the fact that she'd been here, written this, told him how her struggle against her past had ended in this house six years ago. She had killed her brother. And more than likely with Cade's .45.

Had it been self-defense? Had they struggled?

His cell rang, startling him. He fumbled the phone out of his coat pocket and snapped it open. "Yeah?" He braced himself, ready to hear Starr's voice on the other end of the line.

Years before, he'd reached the woman who called herself Grace. He prayed now that he could reach her again in Starr. That woman had loved him enough to want to have his child. That woman hadn't been a cold-blooded killer. That woman, if he could reach her, would spare Andi.

"Cade? It's Carter. I have news."

ANDI DIDN'T KNOW how long she'd been out. She woke sick, her mouth cottony and her stomach queasy. As she opened her eyes and sat up, she took in her surroundings in a kind of dazed, confused state.

The room was small, windowless, the floor bare

except for the rug and sleeping bag beneath her. Off the room was a small doorless alcove that held nothing but a stained toilet and sink. Clearly no one lived here and hadn't for some time.

As she slipped from the sleeping bag and tried to stand, she noted that she was still fully dressed in the same clothing she'd had on yesterday. That alone she took as good news.

She could recall little except entering the bait and tackle shop to close the front door and the light going out. After that, nothing until a few moments ago when she'd come to, but she was sure she'd been drugged. Her limbs felt rubbery and useless. Her legs barely wanted to hold her up.

She heard a sound behind her and turned too quickly. Everything dimmed to black and she sat down hard on the floor. She could hear the steady, heavy tread of someone coming up what sounded like stairs. The footfalls grew louder.

As her vision cleared, she stared at the only door out of this room and saw where someone had cut a narrow slot under the door. The footfalls stopped. In the silence, she heard something metallic connect with the floor just an instant before a metal tray came sliding under the door and into her room.

"Wait!" she cried as she heard the footfalls begin to retreat. "Wait!" But whoever it was didn't wait and soon she heard nothing at all.

Her stomach rumbled as she crawled over to the tray, half afraid the food had been poisoned. But if the person had wanted to kill her, he or she certainly could have at the tackle shop.

The tray held a carton of milk, a small tub of butterscotch pudding and a heated frozen dinner of turkey, dressing, mashed potatoes, gravy and green beans. Beside it was a plastic spoon.

The food smelled wonderful, which told her she must not have eaten for a while. She had no idea how much time had passed or even if it was day or night.

She picked up the spoon, telling herself that she needed to regain her strength. As she ate, she watched the door, wondering who her captor was and why that person didn't want her to see them.

CADE BRACED HIMSELF, afraid just how bad the news would be. *Just don't let it be about Andi.*

"I'm at your apartment," Carter said. "Where are you?"

"At the cabin," he lied. "Why? What's up?"

"Maybe I should drive out. I'd prefer to tell you this in person."

"Just tell me, please," Cade said. He knew he sounded dog-tired, emotionally drained and scared. He was.

"Okay," Carter said hesitantly. "The exhumation took place this morning at daybreak. We wanted to get it done at a time that caused the least amount of interest."

Cade walked over to a straight-back chair that was missing most of the back. He righted the chair and sat down, leaning it against the wall for stability since he wasn't sure his legs would hold him.

"According to preliminary DNA tests done locally, the body in the grave, Cade, is Starr Calhoun."

"What?" How was that possible? He'd heard from Starr just last night at the shop. It had definitely been her voice. "That can't be right."

"It's her, Cade, and there's more. The coroner was examining the body while we were waiting for the DNA results. She was murdered. Like her brother, the slug was lodged in the skull. The wounds are almost identical. Whoever killed her covered it up with the fire, making it look as if she'd lost control and ended up down in that ravine. They must have cut the gas line to make sure the car burned."

The room began to swim. He could feel the sweat break out even though it had to be below zero in the boarded-up room of the old house.

"The slug was a .45 caliber—just like the one taken from her brother's body," Carter said. "We'll have to send the bullet to the crime lab to be positive that they came from the same gun, but I think it's a pretty good bet they did."

Cade couldn't speak. Starr murdered. Starr and his baby. Not Starr. Grace. He remembered the call from Billings, her news, her excitement. She'd sounded so happy. She'd thought she'd put her past behind her, but it had caught up with her on the highway.

"Are you all right?" Carter asked.

"Yeah." He'd never been less all right. Except maybe the day he'd gotten the news of Grace's car accident. Both Grace and the baby gone.

"Maybe I should come out to the cabin," Carter said. "You shouldn't be alone now. Or I guess, you aren't alone. You have Andi."

You have Andi. "Yeah. I'll be okay. It just comes as such a shock."

"You realize there will be a double murder investigation," Carter was saying. "The state bureau will be involved. I've got to tell you, it doesn't look good. I know you didn't kill them. But—"

"Yeah," he said. "A judge might think I'd found out who Starr really was and did something crazy."

"Anyone who knows you knows that isn't like you," Carter said. "But with the money still missing…"

Yeah, Cade Jackson, the stable one of the family, doing something crazy. Not a chance.

"I gotta go," Cade said. "Thanks for doing this and letting me know." He hung up and sat for a moment, too stunned to stand.

Starr was dead. Murdered. And he was a suspect. It would have been funny if someone didn't have Andi.

Not Starr, anyway. But who?

He got to his feet, but stumbled and sank back down. The chair cracked, one leg barely holding as he held on for dear life. He felt as if he would explode. Turning his face up to the high pale-yellow ceiling, he felt the anguish rising in him, choking him as all his pain and anger and fear came out in a howl.

Grace and the baby. He cried for what could have been. The child he never got to know. The life he and a woman named Grace had shared. A life they never could have had even if she'd made it home that night. Grace could never have outrun her past. It would have caught up with her. If not that Christmas six years go, then this one. Blindsiding him, destroying anything they might have built.

Damn her. How could she have done this to him? And now someone had Andi, all because of Starr and her family.

Spent, he stumbled to his feet and tried to clear his head. He couldn't save Starr or the baby, but he had to save Andi. He had to find these people who had killed Grace and the baby before they killed the woman he was falling in love with.

He didn't look at the words Grace had left on the wall. Grace was his past. Her memory was fading like the walls of the old Cherry House.

The voice on the phone last night had been Starr's. That's why Carter's news had floored him. But the more Cade thought about it as he hurried down the stairs to his pickup, the more he realized why the call last night had bothered him.

The first few sentences sounded exactly like Grace, but the rest was stilted, oddly disjointed.

He drove the five miles north, going under the railroad underpass as he went through town to get to his shop.

The tape recorder and tape that Andi had left with him just days ago was right where he'd hidden it. He pulled it out and listened to the tape. He'd been right. The first two sentences were Starr talking to her brother about plans for the bank robberies. The other words had been taken from the tape, spliced together and no doubt put on another tape that was played when he answered the phone.

That meant that the person who had Andi also had a copy of the tape.

He took the message that had been left for him and read it again. All he could think about was Andi. Another storm was coming in bringing both snow and cold. Andi wasn't used to this weather. He prayed she was somewhere warm if not safe.

He told himself that he'd known Grace. He should know where she would hide the money.

Bull, he thought. If he'd really known his wife, then he would have known she wasn't who she said she was, that she was lying through her teeth, that she had three million dollars hidden somewhere.

Why hadn't she just given it to her brothers?

But he knew the answer. She would have kept it. Her ace in the hole in case the day came that someone found out who she was and she had to run.

He read the note again, then balled it up and threw it across the room. The paper rolled under an end table. He started to get up to retrieve it, when his gaze fell on a framed photograph on the wall.

When had Grace put that there? It was in such an odd place that he'd never noticed it before. His heart began to pound. She must have put it there shortly before she died. He'd been in such a fog the last six years, he'd never even noticed since they had lived out at the cabin and never spent any time in the apartment.

He reached to take it down, his fingers trembling. The frame slipped from his fingers, fell, hitting the floor, the glass shattering. He swore as he carefully picked it up and carried the frame into the kitchen to dump the broken glass into the wastebasket.

It was one of Grace's photographs. As he shook off the rest of the shards of glass, he frowned and walked back into the living area. Just as he'd suspected, this was the only photograph that Grace had put up in here.

He felt a strange chill as he stared down at the photo and recognized where it had been shot from—the property where he'd started the house they were to live in as a family.

Heart racing, he pried at the frame. Grace had always dated her photos and written down the locations on the back.

You know my heart, she'd written on the pale-yellow wall.

If he'd known her, really known her, then she'd left him this photo because she knew…

He carefully removed the back of the frame to expose the back of Grace's photograph.

There it was. Written in her meticulous hand. The date, the place and under it, taped to the back, was a small white envelope with his name on it.

Chapter Fifteen

Cade plucked the envelope from the back of the photo-graph and dropped into a chair.

> Cade,
>
> I hope you will never see this. I plan to come back and destroy it if everything goes well. But if you are reading it, then I never got the chance. Which also means I am no longer with you.
>
> I understand if you can never forgive me for not telling you the truth. Just know that I loved you with all my heart. I was never happier than in the time I spent with you.
>
> I hope you will never have to use this because if you do, then I have failed you, failed us.
>
> I am so sorry,
> Grace

Printed in small letters under it were a series of numbers and letters. Latitude and longitude coordinates?

He glanced at the clock. The person who had taken Andi had given him twenty-four hours. It was only a little past noon. He had time if he hurried.

ANDI FELT BETTER after she ate. She hadn't heard another sound from her captor, but she had found a note under the pudding cup telling her to slide her tray back under the door to get more food in the future.

She tested her legs and found herself much stronger. As her mind cleared, she looked for a way out. There was just the one door out. No windows.

The old door was made of thick wood. She realized the lock was also old and required a skeleton key. With growing excitement, she saw that the key was in the lock on the other side.

She looked around for something to use to push the key out. The plastic spoon was too large.

She hurried into the bathroom and removed the top on the tank. The mechanism that made the toilet flush included a long piece of small-diameter metal. Hurriedly she took it apart and armed with the piece of thin metal, went back into the other room to listen.

No sign of her captor.

She dumped everything off the tray but the napkin and carefully slid the tray through the slot under the door. Her fingers were shaking. She knew she would get only one chance.

She poked the metal rod into the keyhole, heard it hit the tip of the key. She pushed slowly and gently and felt the key start to move. *Easy. Not too fast.* Her fear was that the key would fall out of the lock, but then bounce out of the tray and out of her reach.

She felt the key give, and with her heart in her throat, heard it drop. It made a slight thump as it hit. Praying it had worked, she pulled the tray back into the room.

At first she didn't see the key. Her heart fell. But there it was, partly hidden under the napkin where it had landed. She snatched the key up and, holding her breath, listened.

No sound from outside the door.

She started to discard the thin rod from the inside of the tank, but it was the only thing she had for a weapon, although not a great one.

Then carefully, she fit the key into the lock, took a breath and let it out slowly, and turned the key, praying it would open the door.

It did. The door creaked as she opened it a crack and listened. Still no sound. She eased out into the narrow hallway and saw that she was being kept in an old, abandoned house.

At the top of the staircase, she glanced down. The house was empty except for a thick layer of dust. Her room had been cleaned. She knew she should be thankful for that.

It seemed odd that her captor had gone to the trouble as she began the slow, painful descent down the stairs, working to keep each step from groaning under her weight.

Where was her captor? Was it possible the person wasn't even in the house?

She reached the bottom step. The front door was just across the room. With the windows boarded up, she had no idea where she was or if it was even day or night.

It didn't matter. If she could get through that door and out of here...

She inched across the floor, noticing where the dust had been scuffed with footprints. Holding her breath, she grabbed the doorknob and turned, praying it wouldn't be locked.

It wasn't.

She flung the door open, ready to run and stopped short at the sight of the person standing on the other side.

"Hello, Andi."

CADE HAD A FRIEND who was into geocaching and not only owned a GPS, but also knew how to use it.

"You're sure it's easy?" he said after Franklin showed him the basics.

"Nothing to it. If you have any problems, just give me a call."

Franklin had written down basic directions on how to find a certain longitude and latitude.

"Hell, Cade, the next thing you'll do is computerize that shop of yours," Franklin had joked.

As Cade left, the promised winter storm blew in. The wind took his breath away as he ducked his head and made his way to his truck.

Once on the highway north, the wind blew the falling snow horizontally across the highway. He couldn't see his hand in front of his face. The going was slow, but nothing like it would be once he reached the rocky point by the house site. He'd have a hell of a time finding anything in this storm.

It wasn't the cold that chilled him, though, as he drove. It was the thought of Andi and the fear that she was out in this weather. He wouldn't let himself consider that even if he found the money, it might not save Andi.

Snow blew across the highway, the whiteout hypnotic. He kept his eye on the reflectors along the edge of the pavement. Otherwise he wouldn't have known where the road was.

Occasionally he would see lights suddenly come out of the storm as another car crept past. But travelers were few and far between.

Once off the main highway, the going wasn't much better. He plowed through the drifting snow, the GPS on the seat next to him. A gust of wind rocked the pickup and sent a shower of fresh snow over the hood.

He was almost on top of the bare bones of the house before he saw it and got the pickup stopped. Through the blowing and drifting snow, he stared at the weathered wood that his brother and some friends had helped him build. Why had he left it like this?

But he knew the answer. Inertia. He'd been paralyzed by his loss. Until Andi had come into his life. He wouldn't lose another woman he'd fallen in love with. This time he knew what was at stake. This time he would fight.

He picked up the GPS from the seat and turned it on, watching the screen as it searched for a satellite.

"Come on," he said and glanced at his watch.

ANDI FROZE, so startled that the last thing she could have done was run. She was momentarily so stunned that she forgot about the weapon she had hidden in the back waistband of her jeans. *"Bradley?"*

He smiled and she might have misunderstood and run into his arms, thinking he'd come to Montana to save her. But the gun he pointed at her cleared that up at once.

"What…?"

He motioned her back and she stumbled into the house, not even aware that her teeth were chattering from the cold coming through the open doorway.

Bradley's heavy coat was covered in snow. So was his blond hair. She stared at him, realizing that his eyes were no longer brown—but a pale blue.

She felt off balance and wondered if it was the drugs. This couldn't be real. She had to be tripping. Or asleep and all of this, including her almost escape, was just a dream with a nightmare ending.

"I don't understand," she managed to say.

"Don't you, sweetie?" he asked, sounding like his old self. "Why don't we go back upstairs and I'll explain it."

She didn't move.

"Please, Andi, I really don't want to have to hurt you."

She stared at him. "I thought you were my *friend?*"

"That was the idea," he said with a chuckle. "I'm surprised how well you've taken to Montana and Cade Jackson. Ice fishing, Andi? Really?"

He knew she'd gone ice fishing? "You've been in Montana all this time? But when I called you…"

"The joy of a cell phone, sweetie," he said.

"The TV station gossip?"

"Please, you weren't the only person I befriended at the station. I have my sources."

"You did befriend me, didn't you?" she said, remembering the times he'd gone out of his way to talk to her.

He nodded smugly. "It wasn't easy, either."

She couldn't believe she'd been so stupid. "I told you *everything*."

"And I greatly appreciated that."

"You took the research job to get close to me."

He laughed. "Sweetie, that sounds so egotistical."

She was shaking her head, backing up until she stumbled into the wall.

"Andi. You should be flattered. I'd seen you on TV. It was that big story you broke about a woman who killed her husband. Hell, you did all the footwork for the police and solved the damned murder. I was so impressed. I said to myself that woman is really something. And, truthfully, that's when I got the idea. I knew I didn't have a lot of time with Lubbock getting out soon."

She stared at him, realizing something else about him that was different. "You aren't gay."

"No, I'm not."

"Why would you…"

He laughed, a sound that was so familiar and yet alien, that it sent chills racing down her spine.

"As male-female relationship-phobic as you were it was the only way I could get close to you," he said. "You wanted a pal, someone whose shoulder you could cry on, someone you could open up to." His expression soured. "But you certainly didn't have that problem with Cade Jackson, now did you?"

"I trusted you."

"Yes, you did. Now start climbing, sweetie, before I have to get angry with you."

She turned toward the stairs. "Why are you doing this?"

"Can't you guess?"

She stumbled on one of the steps.

"Careful," he said behind her.

"Tell me all this isn't just about the money."

"Don't turn up your nose at three million dollars. Like you said, I'm the best researcher you've ever known. I researched you, found out who you were. Imagine my shock when I discovered that nasty news about your father."

"You used that to manipulate me." She felt anger well inside her. It was all she could do not to go for the rod in hopes of catching him off guard.

"And it was so easy. This obsession you have with the Calhouns…" He *tsk-tsked*. "I just did what was necessary to get a job at your station and get close to you. I had faith in you from the beginning that you would come through for me."

She'd reached the top of the stairs and turned in shock to stare down at him as his words registered. "The researcher position… Alfred's accident—" Alfred Fisher, the station's former researcher, had been killed after a fall down his basement stairs.

"Wasn't really an accident. I just had to open up the job. And Alfred did give me a glowing recommendation before he died, which really cinched it, don't you think?"

She felt sick. Bradley was insane. He'd killed Alfred—after forcing the poor man to write him a recommendation and all so he could get to her? She could feel the metal rod digging into her back. But the barrel of the gun was pointed at her heart.

Bradley shook his head as if reading her expression. "Please don't make me shoot you, but I will since your part is really over. Now it's all up to Cade Jackson," he said calmly as he motioned her toward the room she'd just escaped from. "And you did an excellent job of motivating him, though I was a little surprised when you slept with him."

She clamped down on her anger. He was looking for an excuse to kill her. As he'd said, her part was over. She turned and walked slowly toward the room, mind racing, the pieces starting to finally fall into place.

"My stalker in Texas?" she asked.

"Me," he said with a chuckle. "I was afraid you were starting to get suspicious, though, after all what is the chance of you stumbling across a story like the Starr Calhoun disappearance? So I framed Rachel and her boyfriend. You never liked her anyway."

"And the job in Whitehorse?"

"That was just a lucky coincidence," he said. "I happened to see it. I've been following the Whitehorse paper for years. I kept thinking someone would find the money."

She had reached the doorway to the room and turned

abruptly to face him. "You've known about the money for *years?*"

"You disappoint me, Andi. I really thought, as super an investigative reporter as you are, that you would have figured it out by now." He made a sad face. "I think it was getting involved with Cade Jackson. It took the edge off your instincts."

Her head still felt filled with fog from whatever drug he'd given her not to mention the shock. She shook her head, trying to take this all in and make sense of it. "You're the one who's been giving me the information. Not Lubbock."

He smiled. "Truthfully, Andi, I had my doubts that you could find the money. But I thought it was worth a shot. I knew I didn't have a lot of time with Lubbock getting out soon. After neither Houston nor Lubbock had managed to find out where Starr hid the money, I knew I wouldn't stand a chance, a stranger in town. And Lubbock was bound to head for Montana and screw everything up like he did the last time."

"The last time?" she echoed, although she knew what was coming.

"He killed Houston, then lost his temper and killed Starr when she wouldn't tell him where the money was. If he hadn't gotten arrested when he did, who knows what fool thing he would have done?"

Her breath caught in her throat. She remembered what Bradley had said about suspecting someone had dropped a dime on Lubbock and that's why he'd been picked up in Glasgow just northeast of Whitehorse.

"Lubbock, as you know, leaned toward brute force," Bradley said, eyeing her neck. "You should thank me for saving your life. If I hadn't made that call from your apartment and taken care of Lubbock…"

She stared at him, wondering why it had taken her so long to put the pieces together and suspected Bradley was right. Cade Jackson had clouded more than her judgment.

"You know what's always bothered me?" she said. "Is who taped Starr and Houston planning the robberies without them knowing it. It would have had to be someone close to them, someone really close."

He grinned at her. "Like one of them?"

WITH A WAVE of relief, the GPS picked up a satellite and Cade pressed the page button to get a list that included waypoints, as Franklin had instructed him.

He scrolled down to waypoints, pressed Enter and scrolled down to New, pressed Enter, and eventually scrolled down to the coordinates.

After pressing Enter, he put in the letters and numbers Grace had left for him.

He followed the rest of the steps, climbing out of the pickup, shielding the screen on the GPS unit as he grabbed his shovel out of the back of the truck, and moved toward the outcropping of rocks that had been in Grace's photo.

On the screen was a compass ring and arrow, just as Franklin had said he would eventually get.

He walked in the direction the arrow pointed. At first he moved too fast, not giving the compass time to move. Numbers came up on the screen telling him what direction the spot was from him and how far so he'd know which direction to walk in.

He hadn't gone far when he spotted the cavelike hole back in the rocks. Pocketing the GPS, he stepped in out of the falling snow, imagining Grace doing the same. She would have hidden the money in the fall.

With the shovel, he pried up several rocks that obviously had been moved to the side of the opening, knowing on a warm fall day he would be able to see the cabin from here, as well as the reservoir.

The money had been stored in large plastic garbage bags and covered with rocks, too many packages for him to take them all. Taking the GPS out of his pocket, he deleted the coordinates he'd put in and put it back in his pocket.

He covered all but two bags, which he lugged back down to his pickup. There was no way anyone could have followed him. Or now be watching. Not in this storm.

Now that he had some of the money, all he had to do was wait for the call. He'd never been good at waiting. All he could think about was Andi. His fear for her had grown during the past twenty-four hours.

From the beginning, he'd known she was up to her neck in this mess. A more suspicious person might think she was involved the way she'd found out about Grace being Starr.

He drove down to the cabin, deciding to wait there rather than drive back to town in this storm. He checked his cell phone to make sure his battery hadn't gone dead before he went inside to wait.

ANDI LOOKED into Bradley's pale blue eyes. She'd known he wore contacts. She just hadn't known he'd worn brown ones to cover up his blue eyes. Just as she hadn't known that he had put a dark rinse in his hair. Or that he wasn't gay. Or that he was a liar, a master manipulator, a Calhoun.

"You're the missing brother, Worth Calhoun."

"Or Worthless, as my siblings used to call me," Bradley said with a laugh. "Being the youngest boy, I was adopted by a nice, normal family. But after college, Starr found me. She and the rest of them were always trying to involve me in their crimes. They really lacked imagination."

He had backed her to the doorway of the room. She put her hands behind her, leaning into the doorjamb, waiting for the right moment.

One thing she knew. She wasn't going back in that room. Not if she could help it.

"Why didn't Starr just give Lubbock the money?" she asked, hoping to keep him talking. Clearly he was proud of what he'd managed to pull off and wanted her to know all of the details.

"Don't get me wrong," he said, "Starr was crazy about Cade, but I guess she thought she could have it all, the money and the man."

"Or maybe she knew that if her brother got caught with even one of those baited bills, he would rat her out," Andi said. "Three million wouldn't have done it anyway. She had to know that the minute the bunch of you went through the money, you'd show up on her doorstep to blackmail whatever else you could out of her."

"I've got to hand it to you, sweetie, you do have a feel for the Calhoun clan," he said with an edge to his voice. "But in the end, I will be leaving here with enough money to take care of me for some time to come."

"You're that sure Cade will find the robbery money?" It was the only flawed part of his plan and he had to know that.

"Actually," Bradley said with a smile, "I doubt he will ever find the money. But after the way you charmed him, he'll do whatever he has to do to save you—including digging into his own pockets."

"Cade doesn't have any—"

"You don't really think he makes a living off that bait and tackle shop?" Bradley laughed. "Cade Jackson invested his share of the money his father gave him from the sale of the family ranch south of Old Town. He's loaded. So see, either way, I knew you would come through for me."

"You really do resent me, don't you? All those jabs about you being a lowly researcher while I got to be center stage in the spotlight."

"No," he cried, mimicking the voice he'd used in Texas. "Although it did help when it came to the stalking part of the plan. Me? I shun the limelight for obvious reasons. If you were willing, I'd take you with me." He reached out to touch her face with the tips of his fingers.

She swung her head to the side, away from his touch,

and reached under her shirt to pull the thin rod from the back waistband of her jeans, but made no move to use it yet.

"Come on," he was saying, "We'd be great together. I've often thought about what it would be like to make love to you."

She braced herself, ready to strike. "Over my dead body."

He laughed. "That would be all right, too."

"After you get the money, what then?" she asked, already knowing. He couldn't let them go. So far, he was the one Calhoun without a record. Like he said, he shunned the limelight.

He didn't answer as he glanced at his watch. "Time to call your boyfriend."

He held the phone to his ear, listened, then shoved the cell at her. "Find out if he has the money. Otherwise, make it perfectly clear that he'd better get it or you are going to die."

She took the phone with her free hand, but the moment she touched it, Bradley jammed the gun into her side, making her cry out as Cade answered.

He snatched the phone from her, catching her off guard as he shoved her into the room so hard that she fell. She scrambled to her feet, the rod in her hand, but he'd already grabbed the key and slammed the door and locked it.

CADE DIDN'T ANSWER on the first ring. He let it ring twice more, picking up only before it went to voice mail. He checked the calling number. Blocked. "Yeah?"

He'd expected to hear Starr's taped voice again. What he wasn't ready for was Andi's cry of pain. *"Andi?"* Another cry of pain, then a male voice he'd never heard before.

"Mr. Jackson, do you have my money?"

Cade had to bite down on his fury. "As a matter of fact, I do, but I will burn every last bill if you touch her again."

The man laughed. "I don't think you're in a position to make the rules." The man had a Southern accent. He wasn't sure why that surprised him.

"I have three million that says I am."

Silence, then, "I see why Ms. Blake has taken a liking to you. So you found the money. Congratulations. You and Ms. Blake have more than met my expectations."

"I want to speak to Andi."

"She's fine."

"Not good enough. I talk to her or we're done here," Cade said, half scared the caller would hang up.

"Maybe we're done here."

Cade held his breath, terrified that the next sound he heard would be the click as the connection was broken. But then again, there were those three million reasons for the man to work with him.

He heard a key turn in a lock, the creak of a door and then Andi's voice.

"Cade?"

He closed his eyes, squeezing the phone in his hand as he dropped onto the arm of the couch and put his head down. He cleared his voice, not wanting her to hear his fear.

"Andi. Are you all right?"

"I'm—"

A door slammed. Andi let out a cry, this one sounding more like frustration than pain.

"Okay, you heard her," the man said. "She's alive, but if you want her to stay that way, then you'd better get me the money."

Cade had had plenty of time to think while he was waiting for the call. "Here's the deal. You come to me. You bring Andi. Once I see that she's all right, I give you the money. I'll be waiting for you at my ice-fishing shack. I have a feeling you know where it is. You've got thirty minutes before I start burning the money."

"I'll kill her," the man snapped.

"I lost my wife and baby because of this damned money," Cade shot back. "Thirty minutes or it all goes up in smoke, every last damn dollar." He snapped off his phone, his hands shaking so hard he dropped it.

When the cell phone rang a few seconds later, he kicked it away, afraid he'd break down and answer it.

Andi. Oh God, Andi.

He prayed his bluff would work and that it wouldn't cost him not only his life, but also Andi's.

As he stepped to the front door of his cabin, he picked up the two bags full of money and headed for his fishing shack.

Chapter Sixteen

Andi heard Bradley go berserk on the other side of the door, yelling and cursing and hitting the walls.

She'd heard at least Bradley's side of the conversation through the door including the last part. *I'll kill her.*

Fear rose in her as she heard the scratch of the key in the lock. She backed up to the far wall as the door swung open.

She knew that Bradley's fury could mean only one thing. Cade *had* found the robbery money. But apparently, he must have refused to pay Bradley to get her back.

Bradley's plan hadn't worked. She didn't need to ask what would happen now. A part of her was glad Bradley wouldn't get a dime. But she was now more than dispensable.

Bradley would have to get rid of her. She was the only person who knew of his involvement.

He stepped into the room, the gun dangling from the fingers of his right hand, his head bowed. He let out an exasperated sigh.

"I can't imagine what my sister ever saw in that man," he said and raised his gaze to her, "let alone what you see in him."

She heard the jealousy in his voice. She said nothing as she swallowed the lump in her throat and waited.

Bradley seemed to brighten. "But the son of a bitch did find the robbery money—at least he says he did." He shook his head. "God help him if he didn't."

Andi wondered what Bradley had been so furious about if Cade had the money and was willing to give it to him.

"Get your coat," he said. "Your boyfriend is meeting us at his *fishing* shack."

He picked up his cell phone from the hall floor where he'd thrown it but she knew he was watching her, probably expecting her to try to get away. She got the impression he wanted her to try. Not that he would kill her. Just hurt her.

If he was going to kill her, he would have already done it. No, he needed her. Cade must have demanded her in exchange for the money. She felt her heart soar.

Also she could tell, by the way Bradley said it, that the fishing shack hadn't been his idea.

"I need to go to the bathroom," she said, sounding as defeated as she could.

"Well, hurry it up then," he snapped and checked something on his phone.

She stepped into the bathroom, making a show of turning her back to him. As she slipped behind the short wall, she hurriedly slid the thin metal rod into the top of her boot and pulled her jeans pant leg down over it. While it would be harder to get quickly, she knew there was less chance of it being discovered before she needed it.

She flushed, washed and came out to find him waiting for her. The look in his eyes told her as she pulled on her coat, hat and mittens that Bradley's original plan had been that she would never leave this house alive.

As Cade prepared for the worst possible outcome, he told himself he'd done the right thing.

He turned on the lantern, illuminating the inside of the fishing shack. With the door closed, though, whoever had Andi wouldn't know for sure if he was inside or not.

He was counting on that. Otherwise it would be like shooting fish in a barrel.

As he looked around the inside of the fishing shack, he couldn't help but think about the day Andi sat in the folding chair laughing as she caught fish and he unhooked them and threw them back until long after dark.

All he wanted was to save her. He told himself that made everything he'd done right. As long as Andi was spared.

Unfortunately he had too much time to think, to speculate on who had Andi. He remembered what she'd told him about the Calhouns. All were now accounted for. Except one. A male who would be just a little older than Starr.

The voice on the phone just now had been a male's. Cade had detected the Southern accent. He was betting the man was the missing Worth Calhoun.

Cade heard the sound of a vehicle's engine. He checked his gun, then set it just inside the door. When he heard the vehicle stop, the engine die, he opened the door of the fishing shack.

BRADLEY SEEMED nervous as he cut the engine on the SUV and looked over at her. He'd duct-taped her mouth and used plastic cuffs on both her ankles and wrists, pushing her into the floorboard of the passenger side of the SUV and ordering her to stay down.

She'd sneaked a peek as they'd left where he'd been keeping her, but she hadn't recognized the old house. It was an abandoned farmhouse and there were hundreds of them across Montana.

With her wrists bound, her door locked and the gun within Bradley's reach, there was little she could do to escape. She had to hope she'd get an opportunity once they reached their destination. Once they reached Cade.

She'd hold her fear at bay. She knew Bradley would have found another way if he hadn't used her, but still she felt responsible for jeopardizing Cade's life.

Now she looked out to see that he'd brought her to the cabin. Cade's pickup was parked out front.

It was twilight. The fallen snow seemed to glow. Earlier the snow and wind had stopped just as quickly as it had begun. Now a couple of stars popped out in the cold, dark blue canvas of the sky overhead.

Bradley reached over and with a knife from his pocket, cut the cuffs on her ankles before quickly picking up the gun. "Take it slow. Do anything stupid like run and I shoot you, understand?"

She nodded, more worried about where Cade was and what would happen next.

Bradley released the lock on the passenger side door, slid across the bench seat and opened the door. With the gun in one hand pointed at her head, he grabbed a handful of her hair with the other and pushed her out.

She stumbled in the deep snow and almost fell. He jerked her close to him, making a show of the gun pressed into her temple, as he pushed her toward the slight incline to the reservoir.

The door was open on Cade's fishing shack. A wedge of lantern light spilled across the snow and ice.

She could feel Bradley nervously looking around as if he thought he was walking into a trap. Other than the cabin, there were no other structures nearby—not even other fishing shacks. And what fishing shacks there were on the lake were apparently empty, no rigs parked outside them.

Where was Cade? Inside the fishing shack?

The land around the reservoir was rolling hills. Other than a few outcroppings of rocks and several single trees, there was little place for anyone to hide.

Fifteen yards from the shack, Bradley brought her up short. "Show yourself!" he called out to Cade.

Andi's heart raced at the sight of Cade as he stepped into the light. He wore no coat, just jeans and a flannel shirt. He held up his hands and turned slowly around to show that he had no weapon.

"Let's see the money," Bradley called.

Cade stepped back into the shack and returned with a large garbage bag. He dumped the money into the snow.

Bradley let out a curse. "Where's the rest of it?"

"Inside. Let her go and it's all yours."

Bradley voiced his reservations. "I want to see it all first," he said.

Cade didn't move. "Let her go."

Bradley tightened his hold on Andi's hair, the barrel of the gun pressed hard against her temple. She knew he had no intention of letting either her or Cade walk away. Cade had to know that.

"Either I see the money or I shoot her right now," Bradley called.

Cade didn't move for a long moment. She could feel Bradley shaking with anger.

Cade stepped back into the fishing shack. A few seconds later he came out with another bag of money, which he also dumped in the snow.

Bradley swore under his breath. "I'm going to kill that son of a bitch."

"That's all you're going to see, now let her go," Cade said, his voice dangerously calm.

Bradley pushed her on ahead of him, his hand still tangled in her hair, the gun still to her head. "Move away from the shack," Bradley ordered as he got near enough that he would be able to see inside.

Andi feared the moment Cade was out of the way, Bradley would shoot him. She tried to warn Cade, but the tape muffled her words.

"Shut up," Bradley whispered. "Move away from the shack!" he yelled at Cade.

She had to get to the metal rod in her boot, but with Bradley holding her hair... She saw Cade start to move aside. She kicked as hard as she could at Bradley's ankle then let her body go slack.

He let out a cry of pain, his fingers digging into her hair as he tried to hold her upright. But the weight of her body had pulled him forward. He stumbled into her and almost went down with her, forcing him to let go of her hair.

As she fell toward the snow, she reached down, pulling up her pant leg to retrieve the rod from her boot. Her wrists were still cuffed but she was able to grasp the rod in one palm, her hand closing over it.

Instinctively Bradley reached for her. She swung to one side and rammed the rod into his outstretched arm.

She heard a howl of pain an instant before the air exploded in gunfire. As she looked up in confusion, she saw the front of Bradley's coat bloom bright red, once, twice.

He staggered, the gun still in his hand, as he pointed the barrel at her head. Their eyes met in the dim, cold light and she saw an even colder light in his pale blue eyes.

Andi rolled to the side. Gunshots exploded. When she looked up, she saw Bradley. He had dropped the gun at his feet. The snow was painted red in front of him. He was looking toward the fishing shack.

Andi rolled up to a sitting position and saw Cade standing in the doorway, the .357 in his hands. Bradley said something she didn't understand and collapsed into the snow next to her.

It had all happened in a matter of seconds.

Over the pounding of her heart, she heard voices, one in particular, ordering Cade to stay back.

Men appeared out of the snow, cloaked all in white. In the lead was Sheriff Carter Jackson.

But before he could reach her, suddenly Cade was there, falling into the snow beside her, drawing her to him.

"Are you hit?" he was shouting as he ripped the tape from her mouth. "Are you hit?"

All she could do was shake her head.

And then he was cutting the plastic cuffs from her wrists and carrying her toward the cabin.

Behind them, more men appeared out of the snow to surround the man she'd known as Bradley Harris. She heard the sheriff say he was dead and then she was inside the cabin and in Cade's arms.

Epilogue

Andi Blake looked up from her computer as a sleigh pulled by two huge horses trotted down the main street of Whitehorse. Snowflakes danced in the air to the sound of laughter and Christmas carols.

Her eyes burned with tears as she finished typing and hit Print. The printer whirred. She hurriedly addressed an envelope with the publisher's name on it, signed and folded the one page resignation letter, put it in the envelope and sealed it.

She'd already called Mark Sanders to let him know she was quitting and would leave the letter on his desk. It had been the hardest thing she'd ever done. But her job was waiting for her in Texas. Her old boss had promised her a huge raise and a prime-time spot.

Her story about the last of the Calhouns had made all the networks. Her boss had even sent a special film crew to Montana to shoot her account.

The Calhouns were all gone now. All of the missing robbery money had been returned. Cade had been completely cleared and Andi had done what she could to give her father justice—and peace. There was nothing keeping her in Whitehorse.

Except for the way she felt about Cade Jackson.

She hadn't seen him since the shootout at the fishing shack. They'd both been taken to the sheriff's department for questioning. She'd been sent to the emergency room to be checked out. When it was all over, it was morning and the sheriff had given her a ride to her apartment.

She hadn't asked where Cade was because she knew the sheriff was right. She couldn't ask Cade to leave here. And how could she stay? She would have to give up her television career that she'd worked so hard for.

But Cade had definitely changed the way she felt about him, about her career, about herself. He'd shown her a life completely alien to the one she'd lived in Texas. She knew she would never see her old life the same after Whitehorse and Cade, let alone after what had happened here.

Not that Cade had offered her an alternative. He'd called shortly after she'd gotten back to her apartment and asked how she was doing.

"Fine," she'd said.

"You must be packing."

"I guess so." And that's where they'd left it.

No reason to stay around, she told herself. Especially since it was Christmas Eve and she'd heard there was a big party down at the new restaurant that Cade's friends had started.

But the main reason she couldn't stay was that Cade

still loved his wife. Andi couldn't compete with Grace. And it was just too cramped in that cabin to live with a ghost, let alone the shadow of the house Cade and Grace were to live in together just up on the hill behind it.

While Cade knew his wife had been Starr Calhoun, he still believed Grace had been the part of Starr that was good, the part he'd loved and was going to have a family with. Andi knew he was hurting all over again at the loss of that woman—and his child.

If Andi left now, she could be back in Texas and settled in by the New Year. And it would make Christmas easier since she had no family to celebrate it with anyway. Better to be busy finding a new place and getting moved in.

The bell over the front door of the newspaper jangled, bringing her head up.

Cade came in out of the storm, brushing snow from his hat and coat. She felt her heart take off like a shot.

He looked shy and uncertain standing there, so different from the man who had saved her life. The sheriff had told her that it wasn't like Cade to ever ask for help. It had taken a lot of faith, but Cade had called his brother and told him everything long before the meeting at the fishing shack.

"You can't understand what a big step that was for Cade to do that," the sheriff had told her. "That says a lot about how he feels toward you."

Andi had nodded, touched that Carter had told her, and thanked him.

"I know I told you that I don't do holidays," Cade

said now as he stepped up to her desk. "But tonight my brother's going to ask the woman he's been in love with for years to marry him and I promised I would be there."

She couldn't have said anything even if he'd asked.

"Everyone is going to be at the restaurant—Laci and Bridger—they own the place, my father, Loren, and his wife, Lila Bailey Jackson, my brother, Carter, and Eve Bailey, she's the one he's in love with, her sisters Faith and McKenna." Cade stopped to take a breath.

Andi waited, not sure what he was doing here or why he was telling her this.

"I went to the house site this morning," he said, the change of subject practically giving her whiplash. "I burned it down. In the spring, I'll get a backhoe in there to take up the foundation. It will take a while for the grass to come back in. That spot will never be exactly as it was before Grace came into my life, but in time…"

He held up his hand as if he was afraid she might speak. No chance of that.

"What I'm trying to say is that I can't pretend Grace wasn't a part of my life. I can't say I'm sorry that I ever met her. But in time, like that hillside, I'll come back, too. Not the same, but maybe richer for the fact that I loved her."

Tears welled in Andi's eyes. All she could do was nod.

Cade took a long breath and let it out. "What I'm trying to say is that—"

The front door of the newspaper office opened, the bell jangling as Andi's boss came in. He looked surprised to see her.

"I was hoping I would catch you before you left," Mark said. "I just wanted to congratulate you on that story you did. Saw you on television and said to my wife, 'That young woman was a reporter at the *Milk River Examiner,*' at least for a few days," he said with a laugh. "Best of luck in Texas." He shook her hand and left again.

"So you're leaving tonight," Cade said, nodding as he backed toward the door.

"I thought there was something you wanted to tell me." Andi knew if she let him leave, she would never see him again. She could see how hard it had been for him to come in here tonight, how hard it was for him to burn down the skeleton of the house, destroying the last remnants of the life he'd planned with Grace.

"You probably have to get going."

"No. Please. What were you going to say?"

Cade met her gaze and held it. "I can't let you stay in Whitehorse, not knowing how you feel about your career. I saw you on television. You are damned good at what you do. You deserve the best. I just wanted to tell you that."

He turned to leave.

She wanted to call him back, but she knew the moment was lost. Whatever else he'd come to tell her tonight was lost.

At the door, though, he stopped and turned back to her. "It *is* Christmas Eve. If you're not leaving tonight, maybe you'd like to go to the party with me."

She smiled through her tears. "I'd like that a lot. But I will have to change. Can I meet you at the restaurant?"

She'd seen the dark blue velvet dress in the window of the shop next door. Unless she was mistaken, it was her size. She knew the dress would fit perfectly.

He smiled. "I'll be waiting for you," he said as he pushed his Stetson down over his dark hair, reminding her of the first time she ever saw him.

"I'll see you soon," she said to his retreating backside as she picked up the envelope containing her resignation and dropped it into the trash.

* * * * *

Turn the page for a sneak preview
of the first book in the new miniseries
DIAMONDS DOWN UNDER
from Silhouette Desire®,
VOWS & A VENGEFUL GROOM
by Bronwyn Jameson

Available January 2008
(SD #1843)

Silhouette Desire®
Always Powerful, Passionate and Provocative

Kimberley Blackstone didn't notice the waiting horde of media until it was too late. Flashbulbs exploded around her like a New Year's light show. She skidded to a halt, so abruptly her trailing suitcase all but overtook her.

This had to be a case of mistaken identity. Surely. Kimberley hadn't been on the paparazzi hit list for close to a decade, not since she'd estranged herself from her billionaire father and his headline-hungry diamond business.

But no, it was *her* name they called. *Her* face was the focus of a swarm of lenses that circled her like avid hornets. Her heart started to pound with fear-fueled adrenaline.

What did they want?

What was going on?

With a rising sense of bewilderment she scanned the crowd for a clue, and her gaze fastened on a tall, leonine figure forcing his way to the front. A tall, familiar figure. Her head came up in stunned recognition, and their gazes collided across the sea of heads before the cameras erupted with another barrage of flashes, this time right in her exposed face.

Blinded by the flashbulbs—and by the shock of that momentary eye-meet—Kimberley didn't realize his intent until he'd forged his way to her side, possibly by the sheer strength of his personality. She felt his arm wrap around her shoulder, pulling her into the protective shelter of his body, allowing her no time to object. No chance to lift her hands to ward him off.

In the space of a hastily drawn breath, she found herself plastered knee-to-nose against six feet two inches of hard-bodied male.

Ric Perrini.

Her lover for ten torrid weeks, her husband for ten tumultuous days.

Her ex for ten tranquil years.

After all this time, he should not have felt so familiar but, oh dear, he did. She knew the scent of that body and its lean, muscular strength. She knew its heat and its slick power and every response it could draw from hers.

She also recognized the ease with which he'd taken control of the moment and the decisiveness of his deep voice when it rumbled close to her ear. "I have a car waiting outside. Is this your only luggage?"

Kimberley nodded. "I assume you will tell me," she said tightly, "what this welcome party is all about."

"Not while the welcome party is within earshot. No."

Barking a request for the cameramen to stand aside, Perrini took her hand and pulled her into step with his ground-eating stride. Kimberley let him, because he was right, damn his arrogant, Italian-suited hide. Despite the speed with which he whisked her across the airport terminal, she could almost feel the hot breath of the pursuing media on her back.

This was neither the time nor the place for explanations. Inside his car, however, she would get answers.

Now that the initial shock had been blown away— by the haste of their retreat, by the heat of her gathering indignation, by the rush of adrenaline fired by Perrini's presence and the looming verbal battle—her brain was starting to tick over. This had to be her father's doing. And if it was a Howard Blackstone publicity ploy, then it had to be about Blackstone Diamonds, the company that ruled his life.

The knowledge made her chest tighten with a familiar ache of disillusionment.

She'd known her father would be flying in from Sydney for today's opening of the newest in his chain of exclusive, high-end jewelry boutiques. The opulent shopfront sat adjacent to the rival business where Kimberley worked. No coincidence, she thought bitterly, just as it was no coincidence that Ric Perrini was here in Auckland ushering her to his car.

Perrini was Howard Blackstone's right-hand man,

second in command at Blackstone Diamonds, a legacy of his short-lived marriage to the boss's daughter. No doubt her father had sent him to fetch her; the question was *why?*

* * * * *

*Get swept away down under with the glitz
and glamour of the Blackstone empire as
Kimberley tries to determine the real reason
behind her "reunion" with Ric….*

*Look for VOWS & A VENGEFUL GROOM
by Bronwyn Jameson
in stores January 2008.*

When Kimberley Blackstone's father is
presumed dead, Kimberley is required to take
over the helm of Blackstone Diamonds. She
has to work closely with her ex, Ric Perrini, to
battle not only the press, but also the fierce
attraction still sizzling between them. Does Ric
feel the same...or is it the power her share of
Blackstone Diamonds will provide him as he
battles for boardroom supremacy.

Look for

VOWS &
A VENGEFUL GROOM

by

BRONWYN
JAMESON

Available January wherever you buy books

ATHENA FORCE

Heart-pounding romance and thrilling adventure.

CAUGHT IN THE CROSS FIRE

Francesca Thorn is the FBI's best profiler…and she's needed to target Athena Academy's most dangerous foe. But as she gets dangerously close to revealing the identity of her alma mater's greatest threat, someone will stop at nothing to ensure she remains dead silent. Her only choice is to accept all the help her irritatingly sexy U.S. Army bodyguard can provide.

ATHENA FORCE

Will the women of Athena unravel Arachne's powerful web of blackmail and death…or succumb to their enemies' deadly secrets?

Look for

MOVING TARGET

by *Lori A. May,*

available January wherever you buy books.

nocturne™

Jachin Black always knew he was an outcast.
Not only was he a vampire, he was a vampire
banished from the Sanguinas society. Jachin, forced
to survive among mortals, is determined to buy
his way back into the clan one day.

Ariel Swanson, debut author of a vampire novel, could
be the ticket he needs to get revenge and take his
rightful place among the Sanguinas again. However,
the unsuspecting mortal woman has no idea of the
dark and sensual path she will be forced to travel.

Look for

RESURRECTION: THE BEGINNING

by

PATRICE MICHELLE

Available January 2008 wherever you buy books.

REQUEST YOUR FREE BOOKS!

2 FREE NOVELS PLUS 2 FREE GIFTS!

HARLEQUIN®
INTRIGUE®

Breathtaking Romantic Suspense

YES! Please send me 2 FREE Harlequin Intrigue® novels and my 2 FREE gifts. After receiving them, if I don't wish to receive any more books, I can return the shipping statement marked "cancel." If I don't cancel, I will receive 6 brand-new novels every month and be billed just $4.24 per book in the U.S., or $4.99 per book in Canada, plus 25¢ shipping and handling per book and applicable taxes, if any*. That's a savings of close to 15% off the cover price! I understand that accepting the 2 free books and gifts places me under no obligation to buy anything. I can always return a shipment and cancel at any time. Even if I never buy another book from Harlequin, the two free books and gifts are mine to keep forever.

182 HDN EEZ7   382 HDN EEZK

Name	(PLEASE PRINT)	
Address		Apt. #
City	State/Prov.	Zip/Postal Code

Signature (if under 18, a parent or guardian must sign)

Mail to the **Harlequin Reader Service®**:
IN U.S.A.: P.O. Box 1867, Buffalo, NY 14240-1867
IN CANADA: P.O. Box 609, Fort Erie, Ontario L2A 5X3

Not valid to current Harlequin Intrigue subscribers.

Want to try two free books from another line?
Call 1-800-873-8635 or visit www.morefreebooks.com.

* Terms and prices subject to change without notice. NY residents add applicable sales tax. Canadian residents will be charged applicable provincial taxes and GST. This offer is limited to one order per household. All orders subject to approval. Credit or debit balances in a customer's account(s) may be offset by any other outstanding balance owed by or to the customer. Please allow 4 to 6 weeks for delivery.

Your Privacy: Harlequin is committed to protecting your privacy. Our Privacy Policy is available online at www.eHarlequin.com or upon request from the Reader Service. From time to time we make our lists of customers available to reputable firms who may have a product or service of interest to you. If you would prefer we not share your name and address, please check here. ☐

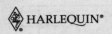

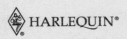

INTRIGUE

COMING NEXT MONTH

INTRIGUE'S ULTIMATE HEROES

6 heroes. 6 stories. One month to read them all.

#1035 TEXAS RANSOM by Amanda Stevens

Celebrated architect Graham Hollister had it all—until one day armed men kidnapped his wife, Kendall. Unless he played by their rules, she would die. But soon he discovers that nothing is as it seems…not even his wife.

#1036 DOCTOR'S ORDERS by Jessica Andersen

Mandy Sparks always had a difficult time following orders under chief surgeon Parker Radcliffe. But when one of Mandy's patients dies unexpectedly, the two have only three days to find a cure—that may be more dangerous than the problem.

#1037 SILENT GUARDIAN by Mallory Kane

Teresa Wade went to Geoffrey Archer's shooting range so she would never be a victim again. But would she find something more than revenge in the strong arms of her stoic protector?

#1038 SOLDIER SURRENDER by Pat White

Gray Turner lived a life of solitude in his mountain retreat—until high school crush Katie Anderson intruded. While his special ops training was suited to rescuing her son, nothing could prepare Gray for the sacrifices Katie would ask him to make.

#1039 SHEIK SEDUCTION by Dana Marton

When business consultant Sara Reese's desert convoy is attacked by bandits, she's rescued by the mysterious Sheik Tariq Abdullah. When sparks fly between these two unlikely lovers, is Sara just as powerless to submit to the sheik's will as any of his enemies?

#1040 AROUND-THE-CLOCK PROTECTOR by Jan Hambright

Rescuing Ava Ross should have been just like any other hostage mission. But when Carson Nash discovers Ava's four months pregnant—with his child—failure isn't an option.

HICNM1207